THIS *THIN* HOUSE

By

Nancy J MacLean

THIS THIN HOUSE,
Published by Fredbagel Books
(Nancy J MacLean)
njmacleanauthor.webs.com

This novel is a work of fiction. Names, characters, places and incidents are the products of the author's imagination or are used fictitiously. Any resemblance to actual persons, living or dead, events, entities, or settings is coincidental.

Print version ISBN: 978-0-9921190-2-7

Electronic version ISBN: 978-0-9921190-3-4

For my favorite children, you know who you are.
And to all my Nova Scotia friends: thanks for making
my years living there so memorable.

CHAPTER ONE

Annie Terrell blinked at her childhood home through the windshield. The weather-grayed shingles and dated windows implied a reluctance to change. Indeed, except for a general fading from the harsh Cape Breton winters, the house looked the same as it did when she had last seen it, nearly thirty years ago.

A heavy reluctance kept her glued to her seat. She had planned to break up the trip from Toronto with a stop, but she pushed on, as unwilling to delay the trip as she was for it to end.

Then she heard a whisper. *It will be all right.*

Annie started at the familiar phrase. She remembered it from her adolescent years, often during an argument with her parents. She had assumed it to be a manifestation of a troubled teen-age mind, as she never heard it after she left for university.

Until now.

She groaned. She had not even set foot in the house and already she had regressed to using a former coping mechanism.

An elongated mewl came from the back seat. She turned around and spoke to the cat carrier.

"Hang on, Temp. Let me see if they left a key for us." Now wouldn't that be the pinnacle of irony, she thought, having to break into the one house on the planet she would prefer not to enter.

She pulled her stiff fifty-year-old body out of her Subaru and zipped up her jacket against a bitter breeze that smelled ominously of snow.

Just as Aunt Jessie's lawyer had promised, the key lay beneath a cracked flowerpot at the end of the narrow porch. Annie slipped it onto her abnormally light key chain, the absence of the keys to her apartment, mailbox, and storage locker a poignant reminder of the end of her life in Toronto.

As she reached for the door a horn blasted behind her, startling her into dropping her key chain. In irritation, she turned as the intruder exited an older model Honda hatchback.

"Antsy!" yelled the tall brunette. Her wind-tossed curls hid her face.

Antsy. No one had called Annie that since high school except for the one person she had kept in touch with: Dette.

The woman reached into the back seat then reappeared with a pizza box in one hand and a six-pack of beer in the other. Before Annie could move, Dette's long legs brought her onto the porch where she set down her wares and wrapped her arms around Annie in a warm embrace.

When Dette pulled back she gave Annie the once over. "Jesus H, I haven't seen yer face in what, must be nearly five years now, and you're as skinny as when I last saw ya, and even then you were as thin as when we chased that damned field hockey ball in high school. A twig you were then, and a twig you remain."

There's nothing better than a skinny compliment for a woman her age Annie thought, and her responding grin actually felt genuine. "A thicker twig for sure. I wasn't supposed to get here until tomorrow or the next day. How did you know I was here?"

"You stopped for gas, didn't you? On King Street? Diane saw you, was sure it was you. She called my cell the moment you left her sight."

Annie glanced at her watch and realized she had lingered in her car for several minutes. No wonder Temp had grown impatient.

Dette tried the door then looked quizzically at Annie before her dark eyes locked onto hers with understanding. She held out her hand. "Give me the key, Annie."

"Key?" Annie feared she had left a bit of her brain along with her soul back in Toronto. "You made me drop it, blaring your horn like that."

A snort escaped Dette. "Lordy, times how they have not changed. You always did blame me for everything."

Annie scanned the porch and feared her key chain had fallen through one of the many gaps between the aging boards. A bad omen, perhaps.

"Aha!" Dette pointed to something shining in a crack a few feet away.

A portion of a miniature gold hockey stick protruded up out of the gap. If Annie had not attached the house key to her chain, it would have been lost in the dark abyss below.

As Annie reached for it, Dette grabbed her wrist. "Careful now. If you knock it through, I'll have to rip up half the porch. Although," she added after a quick glance about, "that might not be a bad thing." She pulled at the stick and a moment later, held the key chain aloft.

Dette was about to insert the key into the lock when Annie tapped her friend on the arm and took the key from her.

It is my house, Annie thought. My responsibility.

Too easily the key disengaged the heavy lock and Annie stepped into a room that, although darkened by curtains and faded by time, threw memories at her. Her sister Kaitlyn, who knocked over that coat rack as she grabbed her coat while their mother's words chased her out the door.

"Now you be home by eleven, young lady!" Then, in a voice so sharp it could cut cloth, "If you're not home then, don't come home at all!"

These words resounded in Annie's head as clear as they had nearly forty years before. She grew up thinking it had been words such as these that had chased Kaitlyn to Toronto.

"I've found work there," Kaitlyn had told Annie a few weeks later. "I'll be back for Christmas," she had promised. But Kaitlyn had returned much earlier, in a coffin. It was on that very couch that her parents told Annie of the fatal car accident on the 401. Annie, not yet eleven at the time, felt as if the sun had dimmed forever.

A dozen years later, it was on the very spot Annie now stood, indeed perhaps the very same oval rug, that, after her parents' funeral, Annie had handed the deed to the house to her Aunt Jessie. Her aunt had responded to this gift with only the curtest of nods, her lined lips pressed thin. The brief hug that followed said it all: I know you don't want to be here. So go. Go and never come back.

Guilt still burned at the sense of relief Annie had felt when she boarded the plane back to Toronto. Back to her studies. Back to her friends. And most importantly, back to Gil, the young professor for whom she had developed a serious crush. That was the last time she had stood inside this house. In the nearly thirty years since there had been two more deaths: Gil's, and now Aunt Jessie's.

Annie leapt back to the present, struggling for oxygen in air that suddenly felt heavy.

It will be all right.

The words, feeling almost like a tickle in Annie's ear, cut through the gloom enough to allow her to inhale.

Dette set the pizza box and six-pack onto the coffee table. "Yer lookin' pale as a ghost. You must be wiped after that long trip. Let's get some food into you."

"I'd better bring Temp in first."

"Who?"

"My cat."

As Annie stepped back outside, the wind stole inside the sleeves of her jacket and made her shiver. When she left Toronto, the trees had still sported multi-colored hues. But here, the perpetual winds had already blown the leaves from the branches. Everything was the grey of the dead and dormant.

Through increasing wind that pulled rain from the clouds and threw it at them, Dette followed her out and helped her bring in the cat carrrier and a dufflebag.

"The rest," Annie insisted to a persistent Dette, "can wait until the morning." There wasn't much else: her hockey bag, two suitcases full of clothes, a few books, and the briefcase that held her laptop.

The moment Annie set the cat carrier down and unlatched the door, Temp stepped out, her fur raised in offense at her lengthy confinement.

"Ooh, what have we here?" Dette squatted down to pet the feline who immediately responded with a loud purr as she wrapped her flexible spine around Dette's leg. "And what kind of a name is Temp?" Dette arched an eyebrow up at Annie.

"As in Miss Temperamental. Believe me, she's more

than earned it."

Dette returned her attention to the cat. After a few more strokes, Temp plunked onto her side and rolled to expose her tummy. The deep-throated purr provided a bit of comfort to Annie and she was grateful she had decided to bring her.

Dette grinned as she twisted off a beer cap and handed the bottle to Annie. "Well, welcome home, ya toad." She opened a beer for herself and they clicked bottles before sipping in unison.

Annie had not had a beer since she could remember, wine being her poison of choice, and the brew's bubbles felt foreign.

A shiver shook her and she knew it was not from the ingestion of the cold liquid. The heat must have been turned off. She waved off the slice of pizza Dette offered her.

"First, let me turn on the furnace." She walked towards the back of the kitchen to the basement door and hesitated at the threshold. Apparently her childhood fear of the darkness below had returned along with the whisper.

She inhaled sharply, flung the door open and reached inside just far enough to feel for the two switches on the wall. She flipped both, knowing one of them should start the furnace.

A bulb hanging directly at eye level flared brightly. But there was no welcoming thunk from the furnace. No heat, no hot water. No chance of a soothing shower. Dread seeped through her. What would it cost to get the furnace fixed or worse, replaced?

She had no money. Only this house and Gil's small pension.

Another chill reminded her of her most immediate need: heat. Maybe the fireplace still worked.

She stepped out onto the back porch where she found kindling and logs stacked beside a pile of yellowed newspapers dated three years ago. Had her aunt stopped buying the newspaper at that time, perhaps because of failing eyesight? Or because she didn't have enough money to continue to buy them?

Another surge of guilt was quickly replaced by memories of the perpetual looks of disapproval Annie received from both her mother and her aunt. By the time she entered her senior year of high school, Annie had virtually stopped speaking to either of them. Her father had on occasion made an attempt to communicate, but that was only to clarify the rules of the house.

When Annie returned to the living room, Dette, her cheeks bulging with pizza, grabbed the paper and kindling from her. "Here," she said, after swallowing, "I'll get this going while you eat."

Annie sat on the couch, wiped her hands on her jeans, and grabbed a slice. She hadn't eaten since early that morning and the pizza tasted absolutely heavenly.

Dette dropped to her knees in front of the fireplace, peered up inside the chimney, then pulled on a lever.

Oh yes, Annie thought, the flue. If Dette had not been there, Annie would have filled the house with smoke. Oh shit, I should get house insurance, she thought. Something else that cost money.

Flames licked at the paper Dette had crumpled onto the grill. She carefully added kindling.

"Good for you," Annie said. "This may be my only form of heat until I get the furnace fixed."

Dette frowned. "I'll take a look at it later. Maybe the pilot light's gone out."

Pilot light? Annie and Gil had always rented and had never needed to worry about furnaces or hot water heaters. Maybe the furnace wasn't even broken. Relief washed over Annie's despair and she was able to smile.

Dette winked at her. "Still rescuing your sorry ass, I see. Take blame. Rescue. Take blame. Rescue. Christ, it feels like high school all over again." Dette looked so much like she had in her teens that a laugh escaped Annie.

Temp chose that moment to tear across the room and burrow beneath the couch.

"Ooh, something spooked Temp." Dette returned to the couch and reached for the pizza box. "You know, this place could be haunted." Her tone was light, but her expression implied that she believed there was an element of truth there.

Her words made Annie think of Dette's grandmother. "How is Gran?"

"She's not that mobile these days and doesn't do readings any more. She spends most of her time in front of the television. She'll want to see you as soon as she hears you're in town." Dette swallowed and then looked at Annie. "So why did you come back? You could have had the lawyer sell the house for you. Hell, I could have done it for you."

Annie sighed. "I had no choice. When Jessie's lawyer called, I was on the verge of being evicted from our apartment." Our. It'd been over two years since Gil died and Annie still had trouble using the singular possessive.

"What? Your beautiful apartment? From what I remember, you two looked as if you were doing mighty fine, money wise. Him being a professor and you a writer. You sold a novel, right?"

Annie shook her head. "An anthology of short stories. Gil had to retire after his diagnosis and I stopped writing to care for him. Not that I was getting much in royalties anyway. Then we went for a second opinion at the Mayo Clinic in Boston. That ate up our savings and, being healthy all his life, Gil had never bought insurance and we couldn't get any after he got sick."

She didn't go into details of how she had taken over the finances and lied to Gil when he'd asked if she'd be all right. He had thought his pension would be enough, but it was much smaller than either of them had anticipated.

"I should have moved into a smaller place after Gil passed, but I didn't want to give up our apartment so I started selling our stuff to pay the rent. Jessie's lawyer called at just the right time. I'm broke, Dette. Flat broke. This house is all I have."

Dette's face contorted with empathy. "Oh, Antsy, what are ya gonna do?"

Annie allowed herself a calming breath. "Well, the plan is to get a loan, fix this place up, then hopefully sell it for enough to get me back to Toronto. I'll have to work, at least part time at something. Maybe teach English as a second language."

Dette touched Annie's arm. "I'm so sorry I couldn't make it to Gil's funeral."

Annie hadn't expected Dette to come since her friend had never flown and driving or taking a train would have taken too long. "It's okay. I was so out of it, I might not have even realized you were there."

The memorial service, after which Gil's ashes had been spread per his request over Lake Erie, now retained the clarity of a distant dream. "I'm glad you're here now, though, rescuing my sorry ass." Indeed, seeing her best friend sitting across from her made Annie feel less alone than she had in a long time.

Dette leaned forward. "Ya know, I did go to Jessie's funeral, hoping you'd be there."

Annie grimaced. "Jessie had given her lawyer explicit instructions not to contact me until after she was in the ground." Not that Annie could blame Jessie. Not once in the last thirty years had Annie called her aunt or written a note.

"So how long are ya staying?" Dette asked.

"Just until this place is ready for the market. However long that takes." Annie waved a weary arm.

Dette took a swig of beer as she scanned the room. "You handy?"

"Other than applying a coat of paint, I can't do a thing."

Dette slapped her thigh. "Well, yer in luck. To supplement my drinking budget, I've done a bit of contract work over the years and I can do just about anything, or if I can't, I know someone who can. And remember, I get an employee discount at Home Depot."

"I can't afford to pay you."

Dette waved her beer and grinned. "Just a wee bit of liquid payment will do. Besides, I'm in need of something to keep me out of trouble."

"What about Beth? Won't she mind?"

Dette used a finger to trace a flower on the couch. "Beth and I split up. Nearly a year ago."

Annie was shocked. Dette and Beth had been together so long that Annie had assumed they would be together forever. Nothing is forever, she reminded herself. The hurt riding Dette's features prompted Annie to speak. "I'm so sorry."

Dette shrugged then swallowed the remainder of her beer. When she looked at Annie, she was once again sporting her signature grin. "What fun we'll have, Antsy, getting this ol' place up to snuff. You just wait and see."

Annie grinned at her friend. "It does sound like fun."

Then a gust of wind sent a piece of something metallic bouncing across the roof and it took Annie's brief flash of optimism along with it.

CHAPTER TWO

Annie inhaled the sharp air hovering over the arena ice and listened to the hiss of metal edges cutting into the freshly groomed surface.

She remembered the first time she had ever played hockey indoors. She was fifteen. Unlike the wind-frozen water of a lake or river, there had been no bubbles, no ripples, just a smooth plane that promised a speed she had never before experienced.

That night she scored the winning goal for her school and experienced a rush that ignited her addiction to the sport. Decades later, the sensation still returned whenever she played hockey.

She gave up the sport when Gil first started his chemo treatments. Then after he passed, she didn't return for both emotional and financial reasons. More than three years had passed since she last played.

Annie stepped onto the ice and, in spite of her lengthy absence, instinctively relaxed into a repetitive push glide, push glide.

As a tall form passed her going in the opposite

direction, a current of concern shot through her. He was quite tall and nearly twice her weight. Her aging body would probably not survive a collision with this man.

Although very supportive of her playing with women, Gil had always discouraged her from playing co-ed hockey, claiming she might get hurt. She secretly wondered, and was pleased, that perhaps he was a tad concerned she might become attracted to a fellow hockey player.

He needn't have worried though. Since the moment Gil first kissed her, Annie had not felt a waft of attraction for another and, with the multitude of female hockey leagues available in Toronto, there had always been more than enough to satisfy her craving for the sport.

Dette had told her about a women's league here in Sydney. Four teams that played every Thursday night. But the cost for the season was over four hundred dollars, which Annie could not afford.

There was also a drop-in practice/shinny in Glace Bay on Friday nights for women new to the game and, like this shinny, it only cost six dollars per attendance. Annie thought she might try one of those practices at some point, but figured she would get a better workout here with the men.

After four laps, followed by a few inside-outside-edge turns, Annie stopped in front of one of the benches and dropped to the ice to stretch. From the end of the rink she could hear a couple of the men talking and because of their low tone, she suspected they were discussing her. Thinking she was too old, no doubt. But the big guy that had skated by her earlier had gray hair poking out from beneath the back of his helmet. If he could play, so could she.

She was facing the ice to stretch her groin when two feet expertly planted in front of her.

"Listen, kid," a man said to the back of her head, "this is adult shinny. You have to be over eighteen to play."

Annie arched her neck to make eye contact with a guy who appeared to be in his late twenties, early thirties at most. His expression of confidence laced with more than a little condescension was instantly replaced by one of shock. "Oh, uh . . . sorry, ma'am. You're so small . . . I thought . . ."

Annie heard a soft laugh to her left and saw the larger man she had skated by earlier hovering a few feet away. His grin labeled him as the instigator.

The younger man skated off, but not before whacking his stick at the fellow's shin pads as he growled, "Damn you, Dooley."

The big man only laughed again before giving Annie a wink that rendered her either a cohort or the butt of the joke. She suspected the latter.

Dette, an imposing figure herself in her hockey gear, dropped down beside Annie. "They already givin' you a hard time?"

"That younger one called me ma'am."

Dette barked a laugh. "They'll change their tune when you skate circles around them."

Annie was not so sure she would be able to do that, as she knew she had slowed considerably since Dette last saw her play.

The game began, dark sweaters against light. They had a referee, an older gentlemen who volunteered so he could get in a free skate.

Annie had put on a light jersey and noticed Dooley wore dark. This provided motivation for her to skate a little harder and fore-check a more diligently, especially when he carried the puck. Most times she was not successful in taking the puck from him, but she did succeed on occasion.

With only two spares per side and few whistles to stop
the play, Annie found herself quickly growing tired. There
was only a minute left in the ice time when the instigator
headed down the left wing with the puck.

Annie skated hard at him, intent on being a proverbial
pain in the ass until he either passed the puck or the
buzzer rang to end the game. He wove around one player,
then another before he discovered Annie was still on his
tail. He spun and lost an edge and before she could react
he toppled onto her like a felled tree.

Her left knee flattened beneath her with a sharp pain.
When it did not subside after he rolled off of her, she
knew she was injured.

"Are you okay?" he asked.

"No!" she hissed as she attempted to stand. Whether it
was his fault or not, the fact that hockey may have been
abruptly taken away from her sent all decorum hurtling
from her brain. Using only her good leg she pushed off
with a myriad of expletives.

A small, distant part of her was shocked by her
language and at how angry she sounded. Since Gil had
died, anger and its many cousins, resentment, irritation,
and others, had popped up at the slightest provocation
but she would usually wait to rant in private. At times she
got so upset that she would go off somewhere to cry and,
oh God, she now felt tears threatening to fall. Here, in
front of people she hardly knew? Just because she might
not be able to play hockey?

"Annie?" Dette looked worried.

Knowing that sympathy would only widen the crack in
the dam restraining her tears, Annie waved as if all was
okay and skated awkwardly to the door leading off the
ice.

Waiting there, presumably for her, was Dooley. The
concern in his soft brown eyes only brought her closer to

the brink of losing composure so she pushed past him as she barked, "I'm fine!" with as much conviction as she could muster.

Her knee throbbed in protest with each step but by the time she reached the dressing room, the ache had localized to the outside of her knee. Maybe it won't be that bad, she told herself.

She could feel Dette's eyes on her, but her friend refrained from speaking until Annie had changed and packed her gear. Then she said, "Want some help with that bag of yours, Antsy?"

"No, I'm good." To prove this, Annie hoisted her bag over her shoulder. Her knee promptly objected and threatened to give way. Trying to protect it but not limp too obviously, Annie grabbed her stick and headed out into the hallway.

The pain intensified with each step and by the time Annie reached her car, she had to face the fact that she was indeed injured and could only hope it wouldn't keep her from working on the house.

As she drove away, tears leaked down her cheeks. She wiped them away with the back of her hand and plotted her future. First, finish repairing the damn house. Even if she had to hire someone. Then sell it and get the hell out of Dodge.

The ten minutes it took to drive home was not enough for these plans to conquer the negative storm brewing within her. Once inside the house, she allowed herself to swear like a sailor whose shore leave had been cancelled.

Temp, smart kitty that she was, halted her welcoming approach and disappeared behind the sofa. Annie limped to the back of the house and suppressed an urge to throw her hockey bag down the basement steps so she wouldn't have to look at it. But as she could not yet face that yawning dark hole and its demons, real or imagined, she dragged her bag out to the back porch and dumped out the gear so it could dry.

Upon reentering the kitchen, she studied the chipped cupboards, partially working appliances, and peeling, flowered wall paper, and knew this room reflected what only a cursory scan of the rest of the house had told her: each and every inch of it was in need of repair or replacement.

After the first walk through, Annie had been tempted to put the house on the market as is. But Dette insisted otherwise. "They just don't make them like this anymore," she had said. "If you fix it up, look how much more you'll be able to sell it for. You're a quick study, you are. You could end up with a whole new career, maybe even have yer own TV show: Handy Antsy."

Other similar comments had convinced Annie to go to the bank. With the equity in the home and her excellent credit rating, she acquired a loan. She was now, in addition to being broke, officially in debt for the first time since she has paid off her student loan.

She collapsed onto one of the kitchen chairs and Temp immediately hopped up onto her lap with an abbreviated, inquisitive meow.

Desolation bobbed to the surface of her emotional sea and she gave into it, sobbing heavily into the feline's soft fur. She could not remember the last time she had cried so hard. Her sobs subsided as fatigue wormed its way into her every pore to the point that breathing, let alone crying, seemed too onerous a task.

Then the whisper returned.

It will be all right.

She straightened up and a startled Temp scooted from the room. Annie took a couple of deep breaths and searched for logic.

Things could be worse; she still had the house after all.

She had a plan of action. Then why was she so upset that she reverted to hearing an imagined consolation from her teen years?

The answer was obvious: just like back then, she didn't want to be here. And, like then, she had no choice.

Then she heard something else. A stream of repetitive, increasingly annoying, ticks. Nothing like the whisper, but worrisome nonetheless. Could a pipe be leaking somewhere?

As tired as she was, she got up and limped toward the sound. It seemed to be coming from the living room. She took two steps into the room and listened. There it was. Louder now, from the fireplace.

On the mantelpiece sat a clock she remembered from her youth that, until now, had been silent. Sure enough, though the time looked to be frozen at ten minutes after ten as it always had, the second hand methodically clicked its way around the face. Then the minute hand jerked forward, making Annie jump.

Maybe when she slammed the door, it had jarred the old house enough to jiggle some life into the clock's mechanisms. Or something like that.

Hmm, she thought. Perhaps the old clock was worth something as an antique. If she got really desperate, she could try to sell it. Which meant she wasn't that desperate yet and just this thought made her feel the teeniest bit better.

She picked Temp up and carried her back to the kitchen to give the cat a few well-deserved treats. Watching the cat gulp down the morsels between spurts of a happy, throaty purr, Annie realized she was also hungry.

Another good sign.

CHAPTER THREE

The moment Annie slid into the passenger seat of Dette's 2001 Honda Civic, Dette waved a card under Annie's nose, too close for Annie to bring it into focus without her reading glasses.

"What's that?"

With an exaggerated flourish, Dette handed her the card. "That, me son, is an appointment for you tomorrow morning at the clinic on Alexander Street."

Annie picked it up and studied it at arm's length. "I thought it was impossible to find a family doctor taking new patients, let alone to get an actual appointment with one anytime soon."

"Colleen, from the Dames, you know, the newbie women's team that skates on Fridays out in Glace Bay? She works in the office there and I dropped by on my way here. Just so happens they have a cancellation for tomorrow." Dette's mouth distorted in an attempt at haughtiness. "Rescuing your sorry ass again, I see." She slid the gear into reverse and proceeded to back down Annie's driveway.

Annie frowned at the card and sighed. "There's

probably not much that can be done." At least not quickly enough. She noticed Dette's frown, and, grappling at gratitude and the more elusive optimism, quickly added, "But thanks. And my knee does seem to be getting better."

Though not much. Even though a week had passed, each morning she still had to force it through a painful stiffness to navigate the stairs and she suspected it would be a while yet before she would be able to skate. Maybe months.

She pushed against another wave of doubt and peered through her window in search of a diversion. One soon came into view. Annie blinked twice.

"The Tasty Treat is still here?" She twisted in her seat for a view just long enough for her to see the "Closed" sign in the window.

"Damn, I was going to suggest we stop on our way back, but it's closed."

"Only for the winter."

"I can't believe it's still in business."

"Yep. Even after Dairy Queen came to town so many years ago, locals still line up at the Tasty Treat on the few hot nights we have."

Another memory from the past filled Annie's mind, but this time she welcomed it. After Kaitlyn got her driver's license, she would often pick up Annie after school, and if the sun was shining, and sometimes, even if it was not, Kaitlyn would stop off at the Tasty Treat and buy Annie a cone of soft ice-cream.

"Now don't tell Mum," she would say. "It's our little secret. And you have to promise to eat your vegetables at supper, even if it's turnip."

Annie would promise, cherishing the secret as much as she did the ice cream. Treats of any kind, especially those bought outside the home were rare, and the cool smooth mass that she tried to hold on her tongue until it melted and escaped down her throat tasted sweeter than anything else in the world.

Annie realized her mouth was watering and she felt more than a tinge of sadness that she probably wouldn't be here when the store opened in the spring. She held onto the image of her sister smiling over her own cone until that too melted away.

Dette pulled into a short driveway in front of a tiny bungalow and turned to Annie.

"Thanks for agreeing to come have lunch with us. Ever since she heard you were back, Gran's been naggin' me to have ya over."

The small house in front of them had seen its fair share of death, Annie thought. Shortly after Dette was born, her mother had died from a brain aneurysm and Dette had been raised by her father and Gran, her paternal grandmother. Then, fifteen years ago, Dette's dad, Fred, suffered a fatal heart attack while mowing the lawn.

But while Annie's house harboured only death, this house also held life, as evidenced by the small woman waving animatedly at them from the open doorway.

Not wanting Dette's grandmother to be chilled by the November air, Annie went up the steps as fast as her knee would allow and hugged the woman everyone called Gran, regardless of age or relationship. Annie swallowed her alarm at how frail the woman felt.

"Ah, Flora Anne!" Gran said. Gran and Aunt Jessie had been the only two people to call Annie by her birth name. Annie had never minded Gran calling her that, as Gran's Newfoundland accent rendered her tone warm and welcome, whereas Aunt Jessie had said it in a way that implied Annie should be someone else, someone better.

Gran pulled on Annie's arm. "Come in, come in. Let me look at ya. My, how long has it been?"

"A long time," Annie admitted.

"Too long! Now, let's eat whilst our lunch is still hot." Gran grunted as she limped into the kitchen, every step halting and heavy.

Annie followed her, feeling instant comfort from the familiar hallway and kitchen. This was the one place her parents had allowed her to escape to. In high school she had spent most of her evenings and weekends here. She and Dette would retreat to the den in the basement, its cement walls, sagging couch, and turntable were all they needed.

When Annie offered to help, Gran ordered her to sit in a voice few could ignore. Gran reached into a huge pot and ladled a whitish soup into bowls that Dette then set onto the table.

Fish and brews. Annie had not had this since she left home. She had never been particularly fond of the dish and always claimed she'd already eaten whenever either her mother or Aunt Jessie cooked it for supper.

So she was surprised to discover how good it now tasted. She suspected the bits of white flesh floating amidst the islands of sodden hard tack and diced onions to be cod. It was, as all dishes served in the area, so hot she could hardly hold it in her mouth, but that was exactly what she wanted to do.

"So you like it then," Dette said. Her grin indicated she remembered how Annie had complained about it in high school.

"It's delicious!" Annie replied.

Gran smiled into her dish and brought her spoon to her mouth with a hand that trembled slightly. "Good for what ails ya," she said and Annie wondered if Gran suspected that Annie had a lot that ailed her.

The meal was finished with tea and biscuits still warm from the oven, which they coated with a generous dose of gooseberry jam.

"I made the jam," Dette said proudly, "with Gran's supervision, of course."

"I'm impressed," Annie said.

"And so you should be." Dette stood up and began to gather up the dishes. Annie was about to do likewise when Gran motioned for her to stay put.

"Do sit and chat," Gran said. "Not long, as I knows you've lots on your plate and can't tarry."

Annie had expected Gran would want to chat. After all, it had been nearly thirty years since Annie's parents' funeral.

Though Gran had sported a more rounded figure than she did now, she had certainly moved about more easily then. She had brought a casserole and biscuits to the post-funeral gathering at the house. But she hadn't come in, and instead had chosen to wait for Annie on the porch.

Out on the step, Gran had given Annie a warm hug. As Gran pulled away, she said, "I canna stay," in a voice heavy with apology. She cupped Annie's cheek with a wrinkled hand and peered deep into her eyes. "Now you go and enjoy Toronto." Then with one quick frown at the house, she had marched down the short drive and up the street.

Now older and frailer, and the blue eyes a bit paler, but just as piercing, Gran studied Annie from across the table.

Around the clanking of china as Dette washed the dishes, a silence stole into the kitchen. Gran took one of Annie's hands in her own and studied it. Annie felt a prickle at the base of her neck and worried she was about to receive a reading in spite of Dette's insistence that Gran no longer did this.

After another long moment, Gran said, "You have love to share, Flora Ann. But before you can do that, you have to forgive."

Forgive? Forgive whom? There were so many to choose from. Gil, for dying. Her parents, for her unhappy childhood and for making her sister want to leave home, thus being indirectly responsible for Kaitlyn's death. Aunt Jessie, who contributed to the former but not the latter. Herself, for not being better prepared for Gil's death and for not coping afterward.

Gran then announced it was naptime and rose unsteadily to her feet. Dette appeared quickly at her side and took her by the elbow. "Let me tuck you in then Annie and I'll be on our way."

"Thanks so much for lunch," Annie said to the hunched, retreating form, moving so slowly now that Annie feared her visit had taken energy from Gran that the elderly woman couldn't afford to give.

Before they disappeared into a room at the end of the hall, Gran called over her shoulder, "Don't you be strange, now, Flora Ann. "

Dette quipped, "Too late, Gran. She's been strange all her life."

A raspy chuckle came from the petite woman, followed by a cough.

When Dette returned a moment later, Annie asked in a whisper, "Is Gran okay?"

Dette shrugged. "She's as okay as an eighty-nine year old can be, I guess." She threw Annie's coat at her. "Off we go now. I'll drop you home before I head into work. And don't go lifting or moving heavy stuff. Let that knee of yours heal."

Annie knew it was more than her knee that needed healing and she suspected Gran knew it too.

* * * *

The next morning, while Annie was frying bacon on the one burner that worked, Dette came into the kitchen toting her toolbox. Annie momentarily took her eyes off the sizzling strips to cast a questioning look at her friend. "How . . . ?"

"Left your front door unlocked, you did," Dette interjected. "Yer startin' to act like a local."

"Just make sure you shut it behind you," Annie said. "Temp is getting more curious about the outdoors and I want to keep her an indoor cat for when I move back to Toronto."

"If you move back. Want me to cook the eggs?" Dette asked.

Annie ignored the first comment and shook her head at the second. "None of the other burners work. I'll bet dollars to donuts this is the exact same stove that was here when I was growing up. I'm just going to have to break down and buy a new one."

Annie figured Jessie must have been really short on money if she hadn't been able to upgrade any of the appliances. She pushed aside guilt that would only compound her already sinking mood.

She pointed to the toaster that was equally ancient. "Want to make some toast? You have to push the lever down hard to get it to hold."

Dette managed to get it to work on the first attempt. She cast Annie a quick glance, stealing a piece of bacon at the same time. "Yer lookin' a bit more rested. Did you manage to actually sleep?"

Annie pulled two eggs out of the carton and nodded.

"And where did this miraculous feat happen?" Dette asked around the bacon in her mouth. "Wait a minute, let me guess. Yer old room, where you were banished on many a teenage night."

"Nope. And in none of the other rooms, either." Last night, tired of the musical bed game that left Annie feeling as if she did more walking than sleeping, she'd hauled blankets out onto the old divan in the back porch. Seven blissful hours later, she'd awaken with more energy than she'd had since arriving. She pointed in the direction of the porch.

"Don't tell me you slept there?" Dette crossed the kitchen and peered through the back door. "Antsy! Have you gone daft? There's no heat out there."

"That's the only place I could fall asleep. With enough quilts, I was warm enough." She didn't mention her nose had felt a little numb when she awoke.

"And what are yer gonna do when winter rears its ugly head, which could be either in a few weeks or tomorrow for all we know. You can't skate on feet blackened with frostbite."

"But I have to sleep. Butter the toast, will you? Breakfast is ready."

Over breakfast, Dette remained uncharacteristically quiet. Her sudden, "Huh!" startled Annie.

"What?" Annie spat out the word more in irritation than in the form of a question.

"We were wondering what to tackle next, right?"

"Yeah, we have so many fun things to choose from." Annie's sarcasm sounded bitter even to her own ears, but her early morning energy felt like it was being consumed along with breakfast.

Dette eagerly leaned over the table. "Let's fix up one of the bedrooms first. Complete makeover. It'll look so new, you'll wanna sleep in it. And if we haul our asses, we can get it done in a few days. Before yer toes and fingers fall off."

Annie grasped at the possibility. "As long as we stick to the budget."

Dette slammed the table so hard Annie thought she heard it crack. "Walls first, just like we said." She dabbed her lips once with a paper towel then grabbed Annie's wrist. "C'mon, you pick the room."

Annie pulled back. "But we haven't had our tea yet."

"We'll do it the English way and have it this aft."

"But the dishes . . ."

"They'll still be sittin' there when you've nothin' better to do. Let's decide on which room so's I can figure out what we needs. Christ, listen to me, I've been hanging around Gran so much I'm sounding like a Newfoundlander. Good thing you came along, me dear. Christ, there I go again."

Annie followed Dette up the stairs, her mood lightening with the infection of Dette's enthusiasm. But this ebbed as soon as they stepped into her old bedroom. Although it still contained a single bed, an old sewing machine, tidy stacks of patterns, and folded remnants of fabric indicated Jessie had used it as a sewing room.

"Well?"

Annie shook her head. "I don't know."

Dette grabbed Annie once more and dragged her over to her parents' room, the largest of the three and the one Jessie had obviously moved into after the death of Annie's parents.

A myriad of ceramic figurines adorned the bureau and nightstands that flanked the thick maple bed frame. This room had always felt off limits to Annie and felt even more so now, filled as it was with personal things belonging to a relative she had never felt close to.

As if reading her thoughts, Dette said, "You know, you could sell a lot of this stuff at a flea market or we could just take it down to the basement for now."

Annie could not prevent a grimace and Dette quickly added, "Or I could take it down to the basement for you."

Annie sighed. "I'm leaning too much on you as it is, pal. Somehow I've got to get rid of my baggage, emotional and," she swept the room with an arm, "otherwise."

They went to the last room, Kaitlyn's room. Other than two filled bookshelves, it lay empty.

Dette grew animated and strode about the room. "Okay, here's what I suggest. We leave the carpet for now, as it's not too bad. We move the single bed from your old room into here. Strip that god-awful paper and paint both the walls and the woodwork, contrasting the colors like I've seen in magazines, sew up a set a curtains, and don't look at me like that, I do sew, and voila, new room, new place to sleep. We can have this done in . . . let's see, I gotta work tomorrow and Saturday, but yep, we could have it done by the first of the week."

Annie peered into the room. "I don't know."

Dette pushed past her and opened the curtains. A meek November sun was trying to push through the blanket of grey. "See, it faces south, so you'll get the morning sun, which is good for yer soul, especially if I use some of that sheer material I spotted in the other room." Dette threw open the closet and its emptiness was so welcoming that Annie risked stepping into the room.

She inhaled. The air was stale but the sun chose then to say hello and set the dust motes they'd disturbed into glittering motion.

It'll be all right, Annie.

This last whisper was as faint as the promise it held.

Still, it was enough for Annie to smile and say to her friend. "Let's get at that wallpaper. I've two hours before my doctor's appointment."

CHAPTER FOUR

A girl who looked young enough to still be in school handed Annie a paper sheet. "Remove your jeans and sit up on the table. Dr. Dooley will be with you shortly."

Dooley? As in instigator Dooley? Nah, she thought.

She slowly peeled off her jeans, sore leg last, and climbed up onto the padded bench. The small paper sheet was not very pliable and she was grateful she had put on a newish pair of underwear. She scanned the many certificates on the walls and found one issued to a Jonathan Dooley. The chance that this Dr. Dooley and the instigator could be the same fellow made her uncomfortable. Although she tried to dismiss the feeling as irrational, it developed to the point she considered bolting when the door opened.

In walked a tall man with short graying hair. His glasses and lack of helmet rendered him nearly unrecognizable until his grin confirmed that he was indeed the instigator. The player who fell on her. The one who hurt her knee. The reason she couldn't play hockey.

He pulled up a stool in front of her and studied her with eyes such a gentle shade of brown they contradicted the alertness residing there.

"Let me guess," he began. "Some big lug fell on you and hurt your knee." His quiet voice and direct gaze tugged at Annie.

Shit, she thought. Sparks. Something she had not felt since meeting Gil those many years ago. She blurted out, "Is that your diagnosis?"

"No." His soft laugh only strengthened the tug. He lifted her heel until her knee was almost straight. As a warm gentle hand began to probe each side of her knee, Annie thanked the god she didn't believe in that she shaved in the shower that morning.

Then he found a tender spot and she jumped with an "Ow!"

As he tried to move her lower leg from side to side, his eyes, now narrowed, studied her face. When he moved it to the right, it hurt enough to make her wince.

"I thought the knee was supposed to move up and down, not sideways," Annie said. "You did go to medical school, right?"

His responding grin created more sparks. Annie reminded herself that after losing Gil, she predetermined that she would neither need nor want another man again. In spite of this resolve, her eyes strayed to his left hand, and, after seeing no ring, she allowed herself a cursory scan.

He carried a bit of extra weight about his middle and to her dismay, this only added to the unwanted attraction. Gil had been heavy set until he lost weight when he became sick. At the end he did not look at all like the man she had married, except for his intelligent green eyes. To her horror, Annie felt tears building.

"Sorry, did I hurt you?" The brown eyes studying her held alarm and she knew the soul sitting in front of her was a caring one.

Annie shook her head. "No, I'm fine." She waved a hand in attempted dismissal. "Allergies."

He studied her so intensely that she went on the offensive.

"So when can I play hockey?"

"Oh, perhaps in four to six weeks."

Disappointment of an alarming strength washed away what remained of her earlier optimism and she allowed herself to utter an expletive that she rarely used in public.

"Probably four," he added quickly. "You've strained your lateral collateral ligament, actually the best one to injure. It's only a minor tear, so you won't need surgery. Unless," he paused then spoke with more authority in his voice, "you re-injure it before it has a chance to heal."

He stood up but stayed in front of her until she was forced to look up and make eye contact.

"Once you do step back onto the ice, you might consider playing with women. Less chance of injury, given your . . ."

"Age?" She welcomed anger and frustration, preferring it to the magnetism, chemistry, or whatever the hell she was feeling.

"Nooooo," he said slowly in such a soft voice that Annie's ire began to melt in spite of her desire to hold onto it. "I was going to say size. You looked like a bantam player out there, and up until I fell on you, you skated like one. But women tend to be smaller than men and playing exclusively with women would decrease your chance of another injury and prolong the many years I suspect you want to play."

Annie fixated on the bad news. "Four weeks. That means I won't be able to get back on the ice until after the Christmas break." How could she survive living and working in that house without hockey? And over the dreaded holiday as well?

"All the better for your knee. Do you need a prescription for pain?"

"What I need is to play hockey!" She focused on her bony knees poking out beneath the sheet so he could not see the water pooling in her eyes.

A warm hand briefly squeezed her shoulder. "You will. Try taking some ibuprofen on a regular basis for a few days."

The door opened and closed with a soft click. She blinked back the stupid tears, as angry at her lack of emotional control as at her situation. She wiped her face and yanked on her jeans, her knee protesting at the rough treatment.

On the way home, she stopped by the drug store to medicate her self-pity with chips, chocolate, and those little glass bottles of Coca-Cola not available in Toronto. Hopefully the caffeine and sugar would provide enough stimuli so she could endure a lengthy session of wallpaper removal that would keep the calories off her middle-aged waist.

She picked up a box of ibuprofen liquid gel-caps. Then on the opposite side of the aisle, she noticed a section of tensor bandages. It probably wouldn't hurt to wrap her knee during the not-fun activities she planned to fill her days with.

Her eyes focused on the braces. One of them looked like it had small plastic struts sewn inside the elastic material, one for each side of the knee. It was more expensive than those without supports, but she decided to splurge. She selected one sized small, tossed it into her basket and limped to the checkout before she could talk herself out of buying something that probably wouldn't help.

The moment she got home she pulled off her jeans and tugged on the brace. Its snug fit felt good. As she walked around the living room, Temp watched her with a wariness that suggested she suspected her owner had lost her marbles. Annie tried the stairs. Her knee was still stiff, but there was definitely less pain.

On Friday night a practice was scheduled for the novice women in Glace Bay. She could go and just skate and not play the shinny at the end. Unless her knee felt really good. Dare she hope? This granule of optimism was enough for her to park her soda in the fridge and the junk food on the counter and head up to Kaitlyn's bedroom to put her knee to the test of labour. If it still felt this good by Friday, she would try to skate. To heck with Dr. Dooley and his depressing diagnosis.

An unwanted recollection of how warm his hand had felt on her knee stole its way into her thoughts and she wondered how a hug from him would feel. She ripped down a wetted section of wallpaper but because she hadn't waited long enough her effort only took off the outer layer. She saturated the inner layer with the sponge so sloppily she ended up soaking her shirt nearly as much as the wall in front of her.

There's no real attraction here, she thought. Wanting to feel the touch of another after being alone so long was only natural. The last thing she needed was to form a relationship here in Sydney, where she didn't want to stay any longer than was absolutely necessary.

She paused in both her thoughts and action. This was the first time alone in this house that her head had not been clouded with dread or depression. Be it the progress on the house, the extra sleep, or the promise of hockey, she felt lighter. Even the urge to flee had diminished.

It'll be all right, the voice had said.

With a more successful yank on the moistened paper, Annie allowed herself to agree with a tentative, "Perhaps."

* * * *

"Sure your knee is good enough to play with the men?" Dette asked as Annie hauled her bag out of the car.

"Yep."

After skating with the women the previous Friday, including playing the shinny at the end, Annie's knee had felt a little stiff but the pain was no worse. Thanks to the brace, she thought, and the regular ingestion of an anti-inflammatory.

"Yer still walking funny," Dette said as she held open the rink door.

"That's because of the brace," Annie lied.

Dette did not look convinced.

"I'll take it easy and avoid everyone out there," she promised. Especially Dr. Dooley. Ever since Gil died, she felt she no longer had to answer to anyone and could do whatever she damn well pleased. Still, she was a little nervous about meeting the doctor face to face.

She was thinking of this when they turned a corner and Dette nearly bumped into the man. He had his hockey bag slung over a shoulder and held a cell-phone to his ear. His eyes locked onto Annie's and although he turned sideways to let Dette pass, he swung back to block Annie's passage. Dette, the traitor, sidled on down to the dressing room.

Dooley kept his eyes on Anne while he spoke into his phone. "I'll be there in twenty, no make that half-an-hour."

Once again, she wondered how eyes such a soft brown could be so piercing. In romance novels, penetrating eyes were an icy blue or a cold grey. She attempted to move past him. "Excuse me," she said and hated the nervous squeak in her voice.

He didn't budge. "You're playing?" To her brief nod, he asked, "Did you get a second opinion?"

After a quick nod and a brief clearing of her throat, she said, "I should get dressed and warm up."

"Yes, you should. I've been called back to the office so at least you won't have to worry about me falling on you."

He slid to the side to allow her to pass, but the narrow hallway made it a tight squeeze and she worried he could feel her heart doing a Celtic step dance.

She dressed quickly, as she wanted to warm up well before the shinny started. After a brief skate, she went down on her knees in front of one of the benches to stretch. Her left knee hurt slightly when she tried to stretch her groin but she attributed that to imagination fed by guilt. Her peripheral vision caught a glimpse of a form to her right leaning over the boards.

It was Dr. Dooley, but to her relief, he stared not at her, but out over the ice, his narrowed eyes fanned by an arc of wrinkles. Abruptly he swung his head about. When his eyes met hers, his gaze pierced so deeply she feared he could read her soul. Then, just as quickly, he straightened up and walked away.

He was gone, but his judgment lingered, and for some strange reason, what he thought felt important to her.

CHAPTER FIVE

The dingle of a doorbell jolted Annie into a sitting position before she was fully awake. With a discontented meow, Temp thumped to the floor. Annie blinked into consciousness as she tried to remember what had woken her.

Oh yes, the doorbell.

She pulled on sweats and socks and hurried down the stairs, shivering in the cold. She had been turning the furnace down at night to conserve oil, but perhaps she shouldn't turn it down quite so low.

She opened the door to a wind that almost succeeded in wrenching the door out of her grasp.

No one was there.

She stuck her head out just far enough and long enough to scan the porch and the walkway. Bare branches danced in the dim light of a newly risen sun.

She shut the door and tried to hug the cold out of her bare arms. She looked at her watch. It was only just past seven. Who would be ringing the doorbell at this hour?

Her more awake brain then remembered they had never had a doorbell while she had lived at home. Had Aunt Jessie had one installed?

She pulled her coat over her shoulders like a cape and ventured outside to study both sides of the door. There was no doorbell in sight.

Great, Annie thought as she shut the door and flung her coat onto the coat-rack with equal disdain. Now she was hearing doorbells in addition to voices. What else was her growing insanity going to conjure up? She stomped up the stairs.

As soon as she slid beneath the quilts, Temp leapt onto the bed and reclaimed her spot against Annie's left hip.

Annie listened to the wind's serenade. She had always loved the wind and it was one of the few things she had missed after leaving Nova Scotia. Their apartment in Toronto had looked out over Lake Erie and she had loved to storm watch, even though she could only hear the wind in the strongest of gales.

She doubted sleep would return, but at least she was warm once more. She studied the room. The 'soft autumn' variant of orange they had painted the walls, the fresh coat of white on the woodwork, and the sheer curtains Dette had whipped up all combined to cast Kaitlyn's room in a certain calm. Annie had slept relatively well for three nights in a row.

Temp mewled a weak protest when Annie shifted so she could reach inside the bedside drawer for the journal she had started keeping the night Gil had died. Each entry was a letter to Gil and opened with, "Hey, luv", her most common address to him.

She sat up in bed and opened it to the latest entry while Temp resettled between Annie's knees. Her last note debated her decision to leave Toronto. Her words were written in a tone that asked for Gil's approval. He had been such a rock for her and had supported her in whatever she had done, from writing to playing hockey. He had made her feel like she was such a smart, interesting person. After he died, her confidence had as well. She felt like a blob that bumbled along in a pitiful existence.

Before she could pen a word, an impatient knock on the door sent her scurrying down the stairs as fast as her knee would allow. She opened the front door to a frowning Dette.

"Good morning."

Dette pushed past her. "Did I wake ya?"

"No."

The dark brows arched as Dette gave her the once over. "You actually sleeping indoors, like a normal person?"

Annie smiled. "I am, and quite well, thanks to your make-over of the room. I thought you had to work today?"

"Nah, called in sick," Dette said over her shoulder as she headed into the kitchen.

These words and a pronounced slumping of her friend's posture caused a thread of concern to twist through Annie.

Dette poked her head into the fridge.

"There's some oatmeal left over from yesterday," Annie suggested.

Dette retrieved the container from the fridge and then began to shovel spoonfuls into her mouth.

"Don't you want to heat it up?"

Dette shook her head as she plunked down into a chair at the table. As there wasn't much porridge left, she was soon scraping the bottom of the container with due diligence.

"Want me to make you some more?" Annie asked.

Dette responded with a muted grunt and a shake of her dark curls. Then she licked the spoon and placed both it and the container onto the table before proceeding to look everywhere but at Annie.

"Is Gran okay?"

Dette shrugged. "As okay as she can be. Her joints are flaring up a bit, as they usually do this time of year. She's askin' after ya and wants to feed you again soon."

"Do you think she would come here? I'd love to cook for her, especially after my new stove arrives."

"I'll ask her, but the only time she leaves the house now is to go to Christmas and Easter mass. "

Annie sat down in the opposite chair and leaned across the table. "Is it Beth, then?"

Dette still didn't meet her gaze and instead grabbed the salt and peppershakers and proceeded to jiggle them in a manner that made them appear to be dancing with one another.

Annie waited in silence.

Finally Dette mumbled, "She called last night." She pulled the shakers apart, then tapped them together several times. "She's been seeing someone, another teacher. She thinks it's serious."

"Oh, Dette, I'm sorry."

Dette pushed the shakers to one side and shrugged. "Oh, fiddle, it was bound to happen. 'Bout time I abandon ship and start looking meself. Though the pickings around Sydney are mighty scarce, let me tell ya." She stood up, hands on her hips. "Want to start on the master bedroom?"

Knowing all too well how sympathy could exacerbate pain, Annie allowed the subject to be changed. "Sears is coming this afternoon with a new stove. Maybe we should move that old thing aside."

Dette stood up. "Then go put yer brace on, and let's heave to, but let me do most of the heaving. You just steer."

Together, with a few pushes, pulls, and the odd curse, they managed to move one corner of the monstrosity out a few inches. Dette peered behind it and froze, her eyes widening.

"What?" Annie asked as she rubbed her aching knee.

When Dette refused to answer, Annie hiked herself onto the stove and peered over the top. She had to blink twice to ensure that she was indeed seeing what was there.

Instead of wallboard stood a brick wall with a huge hole in the center. A draft of cold air moaned its way up from the basement. The sound ignited an anxious cramp in Annie's chest and she found it hard to breathe.

It'll be all right.

Annie grappled for comfort from the words, wherever they came from, her imagination, a memory of the past, or a mind with loosening hinges.

Dette stood back and slapped dust that could be a century old off her hands. "I'll bet you this was once used as a flue for a wood stove. Maybe a coal burner. When they switched to central heating, the installers probably forgot to fill in the hole." She looked over at Annie and must have seen the anxiety riding there. "Jesus H, Antsy. We can fix this without too much cost."

Annie gathered enough saliva in her mouth to say, "How?"

"First, the hole needs to be bricked in. Then we cover it with plasterboard."

"Can you do it today? "

"Ach, no. I don't do brickwork meself, but I'll ask Jimmy at work. I think his dad is a retired bricklayer. I'll ask when I go into work tomorrow. When Sears comes this aft, we'll just have them set the new stove to the side and plug it in." She slapped the stove. "And get them take this baby away."

A moan from the hole sent Annie's chest into another round of contractions and she blurted out, "Can you call Jimmy now?"

"Lord thunderin' Jesus, girl. I guess I can sound sick enough. Where's me cell?" As she punched in the numbers, she looked at Annie with concern. "We'll get it fixed. Don't get yer knickers in a knot."

But Annie felt as if her knickers were already in a knot, and she had no idea why.

* * * *

Entering the rink had its usual effect of righting Annie's world, making her temporarily forget about the house and the moans that emanated from the kitchen whenever the wind picked up which, at this time of year, seemed perpetual.

The first person she saw once she stepped onto the ice was Jonathan Dooley. She worried he would challenge her wisdom for skating, but she received only a brief nod acknowledging her presence.

She had donned a dark jersey and noticed he was wearing white. She considered changing to minimize the chance of another collision, but decided not to because that would put them on the same bench and provide him an opportunity to lecture.

Her knee felt stiff, either from the brace, or from its aging joint, probably both, but she ignored it and went for a vigorous pre-game skate.

Early on in the game Jonathan appeared from nowhere whenever she had the puck and took it from her, perhaps in penance. This only motivated Annie to step up her own efforts, even to the point of leaving her position to go after him whenever he had the puck. More times than not, his long reach and quick hands won out but his ensuing laugh made Annie try even harder.

Near the end of the ice time the puck slid into a corner. Remembering what happened the last time, Annie pushed with what energy she had left to get to it before Dooley. She succeeded, but he was right behind her. Their sticks clashed as they vied for possession.

Two other players joined the fray as, regardless which side was winning, it was always nice to be the last team to score before the buzzer went. Elbows and jerseys were all Annie could see as she tried to find the puck. Then an arm snaked around her middle and she became airborne briefly before being set down away from the play. The whistle blew, such an odd occurrence that everyone froze where they were.

Harry, the ref, who Annie had learned would soon see his eightieth birthday, skated over and motioned Dooley toward the penalty box. "That would be holding, Doctor."

Dooley spread his arms in a declaration of innocence. "Holding? I was just moving her out of harm's way."

Harry chuckled. "Well, it's still holding."

Guffaws echod about the rink as Jonathan entered the penalty box. Annie headed to the bench, hoping her face was red enough from exertion to hide the blush creeping into her cheeks. She fled to the dressing room the moment the shinny ended.

"Hey," Dette said as she yanked off her shoulder pads. "Carla says she and Bob and a bunch of the guys are going for lunch afterwards."

"A little late for lunch, isn't it?"

"Nah. They're going to Duffy's. You know they have the best fish and chips."

"I'll take your word for it. But I think I'll pass. Gerry might make it over this afternoon." She hoped Jimmy's dad would be able to brick up the hole in one visit.

"Well, I have to work tonight, but I should be able to drop over tomorrow morning for a couple of hours. Then I promised Gran I'd bring you over for lunch."

Annie lugged her gear out to her car. It always felt so much heavier leaving than coming. She threw her bag into the back, tossed her sticks in, then shut the rear door. As she turned around she nearly planted her face into the chest of Jonathan Dooley.

"Oh, sorry, did I startle you?"

She squinted up at him through the sun. His infectious grin made her smile back. "You did."

"You know, I was only trying move you out of harm's way. Really."

Surprised by a sudden urge to flirt, something she had not felt in a long, long time, Annie leaned closer. "But it was holding. Really."

He opened his mouth to say something else when Carla yelled from across the parking lot. "Hey, don't fall on her!"

His soft laugh tickled Annie on the inside. He smiled down at her. "You going to lunch?"

With a regret so strong it surprised her, Annie said, "No, I've got to get home. I'm expecting a brick layer to come over this afternoon."

He nodded. "Yeah, Dette said you were fixing up your place."

This surprised Annie. When would Dette be talking to this man and why would they be talking about her? Annoyance at Dette potentially playing Cupid erased her disappointment at missing lunch. She waved her keys. "I'd better go."

"Nice seeing you again." He backed away and the fall wind, more raw now, gushed into the space he vacated.

Annie slipped into her car, grateful to be out of the wind and clear of the pull this man had on her. Forget about him, she told herself. She didn't need a fellow to give her attention out of pity. In fact, she didn't want such attention for any reason.

She was not even fully in her driveway when she began to dread facing the house and its holes and moans. She mentally crossed her fingers that Gerry would arrive soon.

CHAPTER SIX

"Okay, Antsy. Gerry has the hole filled in so why are your knickers still in a knot?"

"And what makes you think my knickers are in a knot?"

"Hah!" Dette plunked down at the table and reached for a slice of toast. "When we were in high school I could tell when something was amiss 'tween us and you've had that same pinched look on your face since I got here. And since you're sleeping better, I figure it's something I said or did."

As she'd never found it easy to stay mad at Dette , Annie decided to clear the air. "Jonathan Dooley seemed awfully friendly yesterday."

Dette's eyebrows arched above a wide grin. "Oooh, has he asked you out?"

"No, was he supposed to?"

Dette frowned. "What do you mean?"

"He said you told him about me fixing up the house." Annie leaned forward. "Why were you talking to him about me anyway? You're not trying to play Cupid, are you?"

Dette barked out a laugh. "No, but iffin' I was, what would be wrong with that?"

"The last thing I need is someone dating me out of pity."

Dette laughed harder which only stirred Annie's irate pot to the boiling point. "Seriously, Dette, butt out."

Dette inhaled noisily and shook her head. "Antsy, it's not always about you. I happen to see Sir Jonathan on a regular basis."

A worry punched Annie in the gut. "You're not sick are you?"

"No, he comes to the house to see Gran. It's too hard for her to go to the clinic."

"He makes house calls?"

Dette put her finger to her lips. "I was sworn to secrecy and I'll thank you to keep this under your cap else he'd be swamped with calls from every geriatric this side of the Causeway. He saw me heading out of the house one day with my tool belt and I told him I was helpin' you fix this place up."

Annie leaned back and let out a contrite, "Oh."

"Oh, indeed. So iffin' he's hitting on you, that's his own doing. And in my opinion, you could do a lot worse. And also, in my humble opinion, and don't shove this back down my throat, you could use a little attention in that department. Actually you could use . . ."

Annie held up a hand. "Enough of your opinion thanks."

Dette glanced over at her, a glint in her eye. "You like him, don't ya?"

Annie felt heat in her cheeks. "What single woman past fifty wouldn't be thrilled with attention from any man?" When Dette's eyebrows shot upward, Annie quickly offered a revision. "Okay, what single *straight* woman wouldn't want . . ."

Dette interrupted with, "Hah! Antsy and Jonathan sitting in a tree."

Annie could not help but laugh. "Enough, okay? Can we get to work now? We have to get to Gran's by noon."

Dette leapt to her feet. "Okay, but I think you should grab any fun coming your way. Are we tackling the master bedroom today?"

"Yep. Last night I packed some of Jessie's things into boxes. How about I bring the stuff to the head of the basement stairs, then you take them down the rest of the way?"

"Okaaaay." Dette patted Annie's arm. "But sometime, perhaps over some wine, you'll tell me why you won't go into that basement of yours."

"I would if I knew."

Dette paused to study her. "You really don't know?"

"No. I just know I really, really don't want to go down there."

"Well, why not try it now, with me? Things have changed."

Too much has changed Annie thought, but said, "Okay."

But the closer they got to the basement door, the more Annie wanted to turn around. Only because Dette was with her was she able to step onto the landing at the top of the stairs.

Dette switched on the solitary bulb whose meager light made the area below look dark and mysterious.

"First thing I should do is put in a florescent light." Dette said. "It'd light up the stairs a whole lot better. There's another light switch at the bottom. You wait here till I go down and flip it."

"No!" Annie grabbed Dette's arm. Only when Dette yelped did Annie relax her grip. She tried to sound less panicked when she repeated, "No."

Then, something brushed her ear with such subtlety she could have imagined it.

So she was not surprised when she heard, *It'll be all right.*

Dette grabbed Annie's hand. "Alrighty, then, let's go together."

Dette's strong grip felt like an anchor to reality and Annie allowed her friend to pull her down one step at a time. When they neared the bottom, Dette reached and flicked a switch that chased the darkness to the far corners.

It looked like a normal enough basement with two small windows, one on the side and one at the back. A utility sink stood next to an older model washer and equally antiquated dryer.

"They might still work," Dette said. "Just think, you wouldn't have to go to the laundromat anymore."

But Annie had begun to sink into a bog of anxiety. She couldn't create enough saliva to speak even if she had been able to force air past her constricting larynx. She knew that if she didn't get more oxygen soon she would pass out.

It'll be all right, Annie! This whisper was loud, insistent.

It felt anything but all right and Annie found herself scrambling back up the stairs, her legs numb, awkward, as if they belonged to someone else.

She lunged out onto the back porch where she gulped the cool air as if it were water.

Dette came out behind her. "Jesus H, Antsy, You okay?"

Annie nodded.

"Sorry, kiddo. What spooked you? Did ya see something down there that I didn't"

"No, I didn't see anything, but . . ." Annie hesitated,

uncertain if she should tell Dette.

Dette's eyes widened. "But what?"

"I heard a whisper." Annie sighed and hoped she would not regret her next words. "I heard that same whisper as a teenager and just now, I heard it again."

Dette stepped back. "What? Just now? In the basement?"

Annie nodded. "And sometimes I hear it up here. But, you know, I think I may have heard it first down there, a long time ago." She had no idea why she thought this. She straightened up, feeling a little foolish. "Then again, maybe I'm just imagining it all."

Dette's frown knitted her brows into a solid dark line. "I don't know, Antsy. Maybe you should talk to Gran about it."

"No! Absolutely not. I shouldn't have told you."

"But Gran might be able to explain it. Maybe she'll agree to come over here and check this place out."

"No! I'll not have her fretting over something that I might be imagining. Besides, it would be too hard on her. Swear you won't say anything to Gran or anyone else. Swear!" Annie was amazed by how juvenile she sounded.

Dette shrugged. "Okay, I swear. Cross me heart and hope to die."

"Do you mind taking Jessie's stuff into the basement for me?"

"No, as long as you let me try out that washer and dryer. They're ancient, but they still might work, and that might be incentive enough to coax you back down there."

I won't ever want to go back down there, Annie thought.

Then, as if in dispute, it returned.

It'll be all right.

* * * *

Just before they headed up the steps into Gran's house, Annie turned back to Dette.

"Remember your promise. You crossed your heart."

"Jesus H., Antsy, we're not twelve."

"Maybe, but we still act it sometimes."

Dette grinned as she opened the door. "And I hope we always will." She turned and hollered inside, "Gran, we're here!" at a pitch that made Annie's ears ring.

Gran stood just inside the door with her hands over her ears. "Bernadette, must ye scream so? I'm not deaf."

"Well. I dinna expect you to be right at the door."

"What?"Gran said as she motioned them inside. "Quickly now, before the cold steals the heat."

Once inside Dette gave her grandmother a quick hug. "You didn't have to meet us at the door, Gran. I lives here ya know."

But Gran apparently didn't hear this either, as she headed toward the kitchen, limping so badly she looked like she was walking the deck of a storm-tossed ship.

"Where's yer cane, Gran."

Gran turned around, "What?"

"And she says she's not deaf," Dette whispered to Annie.

Gran frowned. "I've just put the soup on the table. Sit and eat now, whilst it's still hot."

Annie wanted to ask how Gran knew the exact moment they were arriving, but was afraid the answer might open a door she didn't want opened.

The soup was obviously homemade, loaded with vegetables, thickened with barley, and accompanied by Gran's ever-present biscuits.

"This is delicious," Annie said.

Gran nodded. "Dette has turned into a fine cook."

Dette hooted. "Yeah, with you at me shoulder, else, I'm useless."

"Tsk. Lord knows, yer good with your hands. I'll bet she's a big help to you, Flora Ann." Gran's eyes peered steadily at Annie and gave Annie the feeling that they saw too much. She feared Gran had a sense of what had happened that morning.

Annie grappled for safe ground. "Dette is amazing. I don't know what I'd do without her."

"Oh, gosh, yer making me blush, both of ya." Dette got up to make the tea and Annie wished she wouldn't.

Sure enough, Gran reached across and placed her bony hand on top of Annie's.

"It'll be all right," Gran said.

Annie nearly started at the words and ignored Dette's quick look from behind Gran.

"Sometimes, things from the past helps one cope with the present." Gran said.

Annie sighed and reluctantly met Gran's gaze once more. The pale eyes became unfocused as if Gran were seeing something on another plane. Annie felt equally uncomfortable when they refocused on her.

"Be patient with him, Flora Ann. He's sensitive."

At that moment, Dette set the teapot on the table and started to sit down.

"Who's sensitive?" Dette asked before Annie could.

But either Gran didn't hear the question or chose not to answer as she creaked to her feet and said, "No tea for me. Where's me cane?"

"I don't know, Gran," Dette said. "Where'd you leave it? Christ, sit back down while I looks for it."

"Bernadette, watch yer tongue."

"Ach, you can certainly hear well enough when you want to. Oh, here it is." Dette fetched the cane from next to the stove and helped Gran to her feet.

"Come back soon," Gran said over her shoulder.

Midst the flush of déjà vu Annie wondered if in a future visit she would learn who Gran had thought to be sensitive and what he was sensitive about.

* * * *

Annie hears a noise from the top of the stairs: a scratch of metal. The door at the top opens to a bright light. The brilliance shines around the outline of a skirt. She expects it to be her mother or her sister,and then she remembers Kaitlyn is dead.

More details become visible. The thick, woolen cardigan. Gray hair pulled sternly back into a bun. It is Aunt Jessie. Her perpetually rigid face is oddly soft and her arms extend outward towards Annie, a motion as equally foreign to Annie as her aunt's expression.

Although Aunt Jessie's lips don't move, Annie thinks she can hear her aunt say, "I'm sorry."

These final words, combined with the image of Aunt Jessie looking remorseful, pulled Annie into consciousness. She blinked into the morning light but the image remained in her mind. She searched her memory but could not recall at any time her aunt looking anything other than absolutely certain she was right and everyone else was wrong. She was also certain that Aunt Jessie had never reached for her like she had in the dream.

"Antsy?" Dette stuck her head into the room.

Annie let out a shriek. " Dette! You scared the bejesus out of me."

Dette dangled her keys then stuck them back in her

pocket. "You gave me a key, remember? After Temp greeted me at the door, I thought I heard movement and figured you were up. Surely you heard me come up the stairs?" She opened the door fully to reveal two gallons of paint at her feet.

"Two?" Annie questioned. "You said we only needed one gallon."

Dette grinned. "On sale, me son. A bargain! Besides, I figured we could paint the hallway the same shade. And why you still in bed?" A sly look crossed her face. "Ooh, dreaming of Jonathan, were ya?"

"No. Matter of fact I was dreaming about Aunt Jessie. I swear, I'm getting crazier by the minute."

"Yer probably finally getting enough sleep to dream. Getting more normal, I'd say."

"Normal? I'm starting to say things I never say. Like 'bejesus'."

Dette placed her hands on her hips in an all-knowing fashion. "Antsy, Cape Breton has a way of seeping into one's blood. You'll be saying 'Lord Thunderin' Jesus bye' before you know it. Call it a form of evolution."

Annie sighed and climbed out of bed. "Well, at this rate, I'll evolve right into a straight jacket. What are you doing here anyway? I thought you had to work."

"Last night Chrissy called in sick and I pulled a double shift. I figured you and me could spend the day painting."

Annie looked at her friend with gratitude. "Let's have some breakfast first."

"Sounds good. I can always eat."

* * * *

By suppertime, Aunt Jessie's room had been completely painted.

"Want to order in pizza?" Dette asked.

Annie dried her hands on a towel "No. Let's hit a pub. My treat."

Dette snorted. "And what lottery did you just win? No, a pub sounds fine for sure, but I'll pay me own way. You know, tonight's Karaoke Night at Duffy's."

"Me sing in public? I don't think so."

"Ach, you don't have to sing. But I might." She pulled out her cell phone. "Let me call us a cab."

Annie reached out to stop Dette from dialing. "No, let's walk and put the cab fare towards drinks."

Dette's cackle made Annie want to laugh too. "You always were the smart one, Antsy."

"Just give me a few minutes to shower and put my face on."

"Good thing I'm a come-as-I-am kind of gal," Dette said. "I'll give Temp some attention whilst I wait for ya."

Annie pulled on a pair of cords and one of her nicer sweaters.

Dette whistled when Annie came down the stairs. "Ooh, thinkin' you might meet up with someone there?"

"No," Annie answered firmly. Besides, she thought, Dr. Dooley wasn't really the bar type.

The twenty-five minute trek through the crisp night air to the downtown area passed quickly as Dette and Annie recanted tales of their high school days.

Once inside the bar, Dette snagged them a table near the dance floor, which also gave them a clear view of the stage upon which a small blond attempted to sing Dolly Parton's "Nine to Five."

Dette wanted to buy shots, but Annie insisted on sticking to wine, knowing that with wine she would know when to stop and avoid a hangover. The bar only offered a semi-sweet house wine, which proved tolerable enough if she simultaneously ingested peanuts.

After a few singers just good enough to be unforgettable returned to their tables, Annie said to Dette, "Aren't you going to sing?"

Dette downed a tequila shot and chased it with a swig of beer. "I need a wee bit more alcohol in the bloodstream. That way I won't know if I'm off key."

Near the end of their second round of drinks, when the wine began to taste good enough for Annie to lay off the salty snacks, her peripheral vision caught a tall form standing at the entrance.

It was Jonathan, and he headed over the moment he spotted her. While Dette pretended to study the overhead beams, Annie spewed silent curses at her friend and forced a smile just as Jonathan arrived at the table.

His responding grin eroded Annie's ire and her smile evolved into something more natural.

"It's good to see you both again," he said. The warmth in his eyes confirmed the truth behind his words. She felt a small lurch inside, like a door being nudged open. She knew she should slam that door shut, but the wine had weakened her resolve.

"How are you?" she asked. Safe enough question.

"I'm good," he said, with another look that sent a warm current through Annie. He glanced at the stage. "Do you sing?"

Annie shook her head. "There is not enough alcohol in Cape Breton to make me drunk enough to sing anywhere outside the shower."

Jonathan pointed to the lone couple on the dance floor. "Well, then, do you dance?"

Annie shook her head. "Nope. Can't sing. Can't dance." She had often thought it would be nice to learn to dance, but Gil had never been interested. "Dette sings though."

Dette swallowed another shot and slapped the table. "That I do." She got up and sauntered over to the large binder resting on a table parked next to the stage.

Annie leaned over the table. "She's not much better than I am," she whispered.

Jonathan laughed softly and Annie found herself searching for his eyes. They remained soft and she could not deny the inner tug they initiated. She felt herself blushing and concentrated on sipping her wine.

When her name was called, Dette took to the stage and began to belt out "Delta Dawn." Jonathan emitted a hearty chuckle that exposed his teeth and made the brow above his nose wrinkle.

Cute, Annie thought.

Dette bowed low to the sarcastic cheers that followed her performance. When she plunked down into her chair, she said to Jonathan, "Your turn."

When he hesitated, Annie said, "Go for it."

He studied her a moment, then said, "Tell you what. I'll sing a song if you dance with me."

Dette kicked Annie in the shins, hard enough that Annie had to struggle not to grimace. To prevent another such blow, she nodded. "Okay."

Jonathan scraped his chair back and headed to the stage. He wrote his name down and returned to the table and held out his hand to Annie. "There's a few ahead of me but I shouldn't have to wait for my dance."

A fellow in a too-large cowboy hat began to sing "Rockin' Robin." To keep her shins from permanent damage, Annie accepted Jonathan's hand. His grip was warm, gentle.

"I really don't know how to dance," she said.

He only smiled and led her into a jive. Fortunately, he kept the steps simple and repetitive. Just when she began to feel a little confident, he added an extra turn that pulled her against his chest. She basked in his heat.

After the song ended, the cowboy quickly moved into a squeaky rendition of "Between Two Trees." When she stepped back toward their table Jonathan pulled on her hand.

She shook her head and he let go but the moment he did she missed the warmth and wished she could take back her refusal. They returned to their seats to find Dette had restocked the table with rounds, including a beer for Jonathan.

"Thanks," he said, "but this will have to be my one and only. I'm on call tonight."

"At the hospital?" Dette asked.

Jonathan nodded.

"Do you do that often?" Annie asked.

"Not really. Just when they're short-staffed and have to scrape the bottom of the almost-retired barrel."

The MC for the night, the bartender, studied the book in front of him. "Jonathan Dooley?" he called.

Jonathan winked at Annie and headed for the stage. Following the screen in front of him, he began to sing "Don't Close Your Eyes." His voice was smooth, deeper than Annie would have expected, and definitely on key, at least as far as she could tell.

"Hah, who would've guessed?" Dette said. "The doc can rock!"

Engrossed as she was, Annie didn't remark that this was a country and not a rock song. She only wanted to watch and listen. He concentrated on the screen in front of him, occasionally narrowing his eyes as he focused on the shift in tones. Then, nearing the end, he looked up and found Annie's eyes. She could not look away. He was singing to her. And by the time the song ended, she was forgetting to breathe.

She yanked her gaze away, grabbed her wine, then nearly choked. She was still coughing when Jonathan returned to the table.

"It wasn't that bad, was it?" he asked.

"No, man, that was awesome!" Dette said. "You've been holding out on us, Doc!"

The cough persisted, so Annie excused herself and headed to the washroom. Even after the coughing subsided, she lingered in front of the mirror.

"Don't fall for this man," she told her image. But she saw it was too late. Her eyes held more light, more life than they had since Gil died.

Dette bounced into the room just then and punched Annie none too gently on the arm. "There, am I good for what ails ya, or what?"

"You called him, didn't you?"

If Dette had feathers she would have been preening them. "Antsy and Jonathan up in a tree . . . oh-oh, gotta pee."

Annie suppressed an oath and made her exit to discover Jonathan waiting outside for her. He rested an arm up against the wall behind her and leaned close. "You're not supposed to run off by yourself if you're in danger of choking," he said quietly.

Annie looked up at him. If she stood on her toes, she would be able to put her lips on his chin. "I wasn't choking," she said, amazed at how confident she sounded.

Jonathan took a swift glance about, then leaned closer. "This won't last long," he said just before he lowered his head.

Oh my God, Annie thought. Is he going to kiss me? Actually kiss me?

He brought his mouth to hers. True to his word, it did not last long, but Annie felt every cliché she had ever read in a romance novel, from quivering insides to wobbly knees.

He then took her hand and led her onto the dance floor where a young man was singing "Hey Jude." Without asking, Jonathan pulled her into his arms. The top of her head only reached halfway up his warm, firm chest. They started with the traditional dancing position, her left hand on his right shoulder, their other hands held out to the side. After a moment he slid her right hand up to his shoulder then put his other around her waist and they waltzed as Annie remembered doing as a teen.

He pulled her tighter against him. She rested her head on his chest and closed her eyes, focusing on the rhythm and the feel of alternating pressures of one hand on her waist and the other cupping her shoulder blade. It all felt so right.

Alarm bells rang in her head, telling her not to feel this way. That she was only going to get hurt. That she couldn't take another loss so soon. Then she heard something beeping and realized it was coming from one of his pockets.

He pulled a pager out, frowned at it, and then said, "Damn."

The song ended and Annie knew the night would too.

His eyes grew somber. "I have to go. I'm sorry."

Annie shook her head. "No need to apologize."

Soft brown eyes locked onto hers with a hold that she knew she couldn't break. "I'm not apologizing," he said, "I am sorry I have to go."

He gave her arm a gentle squeeze and then he was gone.

Annie immediately spun around and looked for Dette, anxious to become engaged in chatter, dancing, anything that might hold at bay the heavy feeling gathering inside her.

It was not that she missed Jonathan's presence, though she had been disappointed to see him go.

This feeling was new to her and she knew what she felt was a form of guilt. She and Gil had been married twenty-two years and she had never expected to be attracted to anyone ever again.

But here she was, falling for a man she hardly knew and it felt like she was cheating, if not on Gil, then on his memory.

CHAPTER SEVEN

The doorbell startled Annie so much her whole body jerked. Temp leapt from the bed and tore form the room in a blur of fur.

Annie lay there, listening, barely daring to breathe. It had been a doorbell, she was sure, not a knock. She tried to remember if it had sounded like the doorbell to their apartment in Toronto. But no, that had been almost musical. This ring was simple, two soft, gentle tings of two distinctive tones. Gentle, but loud enough to startle her awake.

Why was she dreaming about a doorbell and why was it so intrusive as to abruptly wake her up?

Annie knew by the light streaming past the lace curtains that she had slept later than usual. She rolled over and peered at the clock. Though it was nearly nine o'clock her heavy body craved more sleep.

She looked outside. Another cloudy day, and colder too, judging by the breeze snaking through the inch-wide opening in her window. She closed it, knowing by the exaggerated effort this took that it would be one of those days. Gil days, she called them.

Still in her flannel pajamas, she slipped on her warm socks and padded down the stairs, her left knee complaining at the forced movement. If she were able to, she'd give herself a hard kick in the rear for letting herself get so wound up by a bit of attention from a man she had just met.

She had let herself hope to see Jonathan at shinny the following Wednesday. She had not. Nor had he contacted her. She had not yet bought a phone, but he could have reached her through Dette.

Not for the first time, she questioned whether her memory of that night at Duffy's had been tainted by her imagination. His kiss. His hands on her back, her waist. That look of regret when he had to leave. Time may have coloured her recollection but he did kiss her, so he must have been attracted to her, at least a little bit.

Maybe he had found out she was financially strapped. Reason enough, she just now realized, for this thing not to blossom. And, since guilt was still riding within her, she was obviously not ready for another relationship anyway.

She sighed. Yep. Better this ended before it started.

The whisper waited for her in the living room.

It will be all right.

"How can you say that?" Annie swung about, searching for something, anything that would tell her that the voice was not a sign she was going insane. "What makes you so sure?" she yelled to the room, to the house.

The only answer was the gentle ticking of the clock, four hours and twenty minutes off the actual time. Annie had no clue how to reset it. She shivered at the cold air enveloping her and another worry nudged its way into her head: the furnace could be struggling to keep up with the dropping temperatures. Hopefully it wouldn't suffer an expensive demise before she put the house on the market. She reluctantly returned up the stairs for a sweater.

Annie picked up a discarded sweater off the floor and eyed the worn carpet. Once a vibrant maroon, it had faded to an ugly shade of dark pink. Replacing it was on her to-do list. But she didn't want to pull the carpets up in the other two bedrooms until the walls were done.

A distant memory of having to sleep downstairs because her parents were re-varnishing the upstairs hardwood floors trickled into Annie's brain and she wondered about the state of the wood lying beneath the carpet.

To make any damage she was about to inflict less obvious, she picked a spot behind the door. With a little prying and a lot of cursing, she managed to lift up one corner. When she had enough to grab hold of, she yanked with both hands. With a sickening tearing sound, a piece of the carpet came off, bringing with it a small cloud of dust.

Beneath the carpet she found a layer of yellow foam. With more effort, she managed to expose a sliver of wood.

She leaned back on her heels, already exhausted. She had achieved nothing but a mess that would probably cost her more to fix than if she had left the damn thing alone in the first place.

Maybe a better plan would be to spend the morning in bed with a cup of tea and a novel. But the books she got from the library all had a romance theme and most of the scenes would trigger a recollection of what she now called "The Kiss." She wondered what had occupied her mind before that night at the pub.

The answer was never far away and most often just around the corner: Gil's death. Kind, generous, supportive Gil and his premature, painful death. A tsunami of emotion forced her back onto the bed. Gil. Oh my God, Gil. Are you really gone? She hugged herself and rocked back and forth, trying to stem the surging sobs.

It will be all right, Annie.

"It is not all right!" She screamed to the walls. "It will never be all right!" To punctuate this, she picked up a book off the night table and threw it against the opposite wall, then swore at the wound she had created in the new paint.

Good God! She was losing it. Really losing it. She ran down the stairs, grabbed her coat, fumbled into her sneakers and, as she had so many times in her past, fled her childhood home. It didn't matter if her knee was sore. Or that she still had her pajamas on. She dared anyone to comment on her attire. Then at least her anger would have a target.

She burst outside. The clouds were making good on their threat, as it had begun to snow heavily. In spite of the slickness to the sidewalk, Annie began to run hard, ignoring the stabbing pain in her knee. She sucked the crisp air into lungs that fought the forced expansion.

She hadn't jogged in some time and was soon out of breath. She spotted a corner store in the distance. Maybe some junk food to accompany the reading of the trashiest novel she could find would lift her mood.

As she approached the store, she realized her anger had abated somewhat. And the air felt lighter. Maybe if she ran more often, she could hold onto sanity a little longer. At least until she moved back to where she belonged.

She noticed then that everything about her wore a coat of winter's white. Even the electrical and telephone wires. It reminded Annie that Christmas was mere weeks away. She had spent that first Christmas without Gil with their closest friends whose good intentions only made the season harder. Last year, she had lied to everyone. She let them all think she was visiting one of the others. No doubt they had figured out her lies, but none of them had called her on them. She ended up spending most of the worst day of the year in bed sleeping off the bottle of wine she had medicated herself with the night before.

She forced herself to look ahead, not back. First, junk food and a juicy novel and then, before the sugar rush began its downhill spiral, she would drive to Home Depot and consult Dette on what to do with the carpet. A search of her pockets rewarded her with a five-dollar bill and some change.

She hesitated outside the door of the store. No doubt her attire rendered her a homeless person. But she ignorned this and flung open the store door with confidence. She paused at the threshold when she caught a glimpse of a public phone on the outside corner of the store. She could call Dette and ask her about the carpet.

Or . . . she could call the clinic and see if Jonathan had an opening. She could make the appointment on the pretense of getting her knee checked. Seeing him face to face might help her see things more realistically. Help her erase the magic of The Kiss. Or at least give him a chance to say he made a mistake.

Before she did another mental flip-flop, she let the door close and jogged over to the phone. She leaned between the plastic sides in an effort to keep her face protected from an increasing wind that now pushed the falling snow at an angle.

The chain dangled empty. She deposited a quarter and pushed the zero button and when the operator answered, she sputtered, "Alexander Medical Clinic."

Soon she was connected to the desk at the clinic. Expecting Colleen from the women's hockey team, she

was surprised when another woman answered. Annie
stuttered, then tried again. "Would – would Dr. Dooley
be in?"

"Yes, would you like an appointment?"

Annie swallowed the lump in her throat. "Uh . . ."

"We've had cancellations today because of the
weather. And we may be closing early. Let's see . . . can
you get here in half an hour?"

"Uh . . .yeah." Her knee had been feeling better. At
least before today's run. But he didn't need to know
either of these facts. As an aside, she could ask why he
hadn't been at hockey without coming across as some
kind of stalker. She startled when she realized the
receptionist was speaking. "I'm sorry, what did you say?"

"Your name, dear. I need your name."

"Terrell. Annie Terrell." Bond. James Bond.

"See you in half an hour, then."

Annie glanced at her watch. She figured she must have
run at least ten minutes. Ten minutes to get back home
and another fifteen to drive to the clinic, probably longer
in this weather. That left five minutes to shower and add
a minimum of makeup.

Knowing she would soon be seeing Jonathan changed
the chemistry in her body. Or at least it felt that way. The
run home took a total of six minutes and it felt effortless.
She allowed the extra time to primp in front of the
mirror. As she threw on a clean pair of jeans and a
sweatshirt, doubt grew within her.

"What are you doing?" she asked herself as she
whipped off the sweatshirt and donned instead a black
blouse. She should probably call and cancel. She would, if
she had a phone.

Annie shook her head as she ran down the stairs.
Maybe it was good Dette was so busy working these days.
That way there was no witness to her obvious mental

deterioration.

She bounded to the door, more energized than she had felt in some time.

CHAPTER EIGHT

Annie wiggled her bare feet in the air as she sat atop the padded bench, the small paper sheet over her knees. Déjà vu, she thought. She debated on the first thing she would say to Jonathan. "You weren't at shinny." The truth. "My knee has started giving me a little trouble." A lie. In fact, her knee felt pretty good even after her run this morning.

But as the seconds ticked away, she became progressively more certain that she shouldn't have come, that this thing could have met its demise without this encounter. She considered pulling on her jeans and escaping when the door opened. She caught her breath and tried to appear relaxed.

All effort was abandoned when a tall blond woman entered the room.

"Oh," Annie gushed. "I thought I was going to see Dr. Dooley."

The woman smiled and her eyes crinkled in a familiar way. "I am Dr. Dooley. Sara Dooley. Were you expecting to see my father?"

Oh shit, Annie thought. Her face must have revealed the answer, as the young woman smiled and pulled up a stool. She studied the chart in her hand.

"I see you saw my dad about a knee injury?" She glanced at Annie's bony knees poking out beneath the sheet then back at the chart. "It was the left one, wasn't it?"

"Uh, yeah." Before Annie could say anything else, the too-efficient woman poked and moved her knee the same way her dad had done, only it had hurt then. There was no pain now.

"That doesn't hurt?" she asked.

"No," Annie blurted out. "I wanted to make sure it was okay to play hockey." Her cheeks burned with her effort at subterfuge.

"You play hockey?" she asked as if pleasantly surprised. "Good for you." She consulted the chart again. "Let's see, it's been almost four weeks since you injured it, and though your lateral ligament feels a little lax, you should be able to skate okay. Wouldn't hurt to do some strengthening. Do you want a referral for physiotherapy or do you want to go to a gym and use the machines there?"

Instead of confessing that she could not afford to go to either, Annie said, "Uh, I don't need the referral, thanks."

To Annie's relief, Dr. Sara stood up and moved toward the door. There she paused. "My dad plays hockey, too. Did he mention that to you?"

Annie only nodded, then reached for her jeans as if she was in a hurry. She was relieved to hear the door close.

"Stupid, stupid, stupid!" Annie muttered to herself as she yanked on her jeans and laced up her sneakers. All that had to happen for her to look like a stalker was for her name to come up in casual conversation between the two Dr. Dooleys.

She hurried through the now empty waiting room and headed outside, hauling her hood against the snow that had evolved into hard pellets. She lowered her head against the elements and turned towards her car, nearly colliding with a tall form.

"Annie?"

The man she had fabricated a lie to see peered out from beneath a hat brim pulled low. He took her elbow and gently led her back to the doorway beneath the small overhang. There, he nudged her into the corner and stood in front of her. She was protected from the storm but she could see the lower hem of his coat move with the wind and could hear the snow bounce off his back.

He stayed silent until she brought her eyes up to his. They held honest concern. "You okay?" He cast a quick glance over his shoulder at the clinic door.

Annie discovered she had lost the ability to form words. She attempted to wave nonchalantly, but her movements felt awkward, broken, like her tongue.

"Oh," she finally managed to gush, "woman stuff." Oh shit. She had gone from being desperate to having anything from a bladder infection to vaginal dryness, maybe even an STD. She waved again, as if the movement could erase her words. "I'm fine!" Her laugh sounded like it too needed to be fixed.

He smiled, the humor reaching his eyes. She searched for the reasons she had wanted to see him. Oh yeah, to see if she had imagined her attraction to him. That's a definite *no*, she thought, then remembered she had convinced herself that it would be better if this thing ended here. She hoped that he would tell her that he'd been trying to avoid her, and the kiss had been a mistake. But his next words told her otherwise.

"I was out of town and didn't get home until last night. How was shinny?"

The power of speech returned to her. "Fun. No one fell on me."

She drank in his soft laugh. He took a quick glance about, removed his hat and leaned towards her, casting her once more into a world that did not seem real. His kiss was soft, gentle, accepting, and it completely pushed from Annie's mind all the reasons why this should end.

When he pulled back, she grasped for sanity through the offensive route. "You, Dr. Dooley, have a fetish for kissing in public."

"No," he said softly, deliberately. "I have a fetish for kissing you."

They stood close, their coats touching. Annie yearned to lean against him.

"You know," he said, "there was a smart fella from Baddeck who invented this thingy that allows people to call one another. Then, another smart man invented a thingamabob that could send mail through the ethernet."

A laugh escaped her and it sounded nearly normal. "I haven't had either connected yet." Because she couldn't really afford to. Would this well-to-do doctor want to see her again if he knew this? Should she say something now and pre-empt his future rejection?

Before she could decide, he pulled out a card from his wallet and scribbled on it. "If you get connected soon, here's my email and cell info." As he shoved both pen and wallet back inside his jacket, he nodded back at the clinic door. "I'd better get in there. Drive carefully going home; the roads are slick."

"You too," she said.

Then he was gone, making her realize his departures had always been as abrupt as his appearances. Was this a reflection of how their relationship would be? Should she just bail now, and protect herself from being hurt? Then at least her independence that had come at such a cost would be safe. She glanced briefly at his card before slipping it into her pocket with an uncertain sigh.

She drove home with the same conflicting, worrying emotions that had brought her. The only thing she had achieved was confirmation that she was indeed attracted to the man and he obviously to her. And that scared her more than anything.

She pulled into her driveway and discovered Dette's old Honda parked there. She found her friend in the kitchen, a beer in front of her, a piece of pizza in her hand, and Temp curled on her lap.

Dette waved a limp slice. "I was famished, so I started without you."

"Aren't you supposed to be working?"

Dette took a gulp of beer and then said, "Nice to see you too, Farley. The store closed early, with the crappy weather and all, and Gran's having a good day, so I figured I could be of some use here."

As there was no wine left in the house, Annie opened a beer and drained half of it before a burp escaped. "I think I may need something stronger."

Dette took the beer from her, finished it off, and then belched so loud and long Annie thought it could serve as a foghorn. Dette pointed her finger at Annie. "Now, *that's* a burp. Why do you need something stronger? Where were you?"

Annie sank into the opposite chair. "Making a complete ass of myself." She told Dette everything, including running into Jonathan outside.

Dette chortled. "Antsy, I'm so proud of you," she said with such sincerity that it made Annie laugh. Then Dette's subsequent giggles unleashed ones from deep inside Annie, the place where all sobs and laughs lived together and battled each other to see which got to surface first.

Finally they both subsided into a kindred silence. "Shit, Dette," Annie said, "I'm afraid I'm really losing it. Twice now a doorbell has woken me up in the morning, and this frigging house doesn't even have a doorbell!"

Dette paused with her beer in the air. "A doorbell? Really? You sure Jessie didn't have one installed, maybe in a weird place?"

"The first time I got up and looked, no one was there. And then I looked for the damn doorbell. It doesn't exist."

Dette frowned thoughtfully. "Hmm, maybe you're just dreaming it, but repetitive dreams usually mean something."

Annie waved her arms in exasperation. "What could the ring of a doorbell possibly mean?"

Dette thought a moment, then shrugged. "What does someone usually want when they ring the doorbell?" She waited until Annie threw her hands up in exasperation.

"They want you to open the door! Or, maybe in this case, they want you to open a certain door." Dette smugly swilled more beer.

Annie frowned at her friend. "And what is that supposed to mean?"

"Ansty, something or someone is telling you to open a door, as in move on. You know the saying, when one door closes, another one opens. Well, maybe there's a door opening for you and you ain't going through it like yer supposed to."

Annie sighed. "Well, I think I'm just going nuts. I'm hearing doorbells that don't exist and whispers no one else hears. I've even resorted to stalking a man I hardly know.

"Yep, yer looney," Dette said with a grin.

Annie nodded. "Certifiable."

"Cracker jacks," Dette added.

Annie laughed and punched Dette in the arm. "That's enough."

"Porridge for brains."

"Enough!"

"Fig Newton with a squishy fig." Dette pulled the tab on another beer.

Annie picked up an empty can and chucked it at her friend who used the pizza box as a shield.

"You're making me deform the pizza," Dette said.

"Then let's call a truce and eat the damn thing. It must be getting cold."

Cold or not, it was delicious and they managed to finish the whole thing off.

"Tell me about this whisper of yours," Dette asked as she licked sauce off her fingers. "Male or female?"

Already regretting she had brought up the whisper again, Annie answered, "Female," though she had no idea why she thought this.

"Maybe she's a ghost," Dette said.

"Right." Annie could feel a thread of fear snaking through her sarcasm. She listened, but all she could hear was the soft purr coming from Dette's lap. And the tick of that damn antique clock on the mantelpiece.

"Maybe I should mention both it and the doorbell dream to Gran," Dette suggested.

"No! She might want to come over here and do a séance or something. And that would be too hard on her. Besides, it's all probably just in my head. Porridge for brains."

"Gran does want to see you again soon. Saying you'll come for Christmas dinner will appease her, for now."

"But, Dette, you said she's frail. I don't want her going to a lot of bother . . ."

Dette cut her off with a wave of a beer can. "Any real bother will fall on my shoulders and you shouldn't deny a woman in a frail state any anticipation that will most likely energize her from now until the New Year."

The dreaded season was still a few weeks away and perhaps Annie would have made enough progress on the house to have the end in sight. Maybe, just maybe, this would put her in a frame of mind different from recent Christmases.

Annie sighed then uttered, "Okay."

A resounding "Yes!" from Dette sent Temp fleeing from her lap. "Gran will be thrilled!" Dette wiped her face with a piece of paper towel and stood up. "By the way, I'll be picking you up tomorrow night at seven. Have your hockey bag ready."

"There's no practice on Thursdays."

"I've signed you up for my team in the league. We're also called the Dames."

"Dette, you know I can't afford to play in the league."

"I paid for you. This way I'll have someone to travel to the games with."

"I know you mean well, Dette, but I have to learn to live within my means, and right now, I just can't afford league hockey."

Dette wagged a finger in Annie's face. "Now I knows you hates taking and would rather give, but give a little by letting me do this, Antsy. Please?" She planted herself in front of Annie. "I didn't have to pay the whole amount as you've missed a third of the season, so it wasn't that much."

"Dette, thanks for offering, but . . ."

"No buts. It's done. If you don't show up, me money will be wasted. C'mon, Antsy, think of what fun we'll have, playing on the same team for the first time in more than thirty years."

Annie sighed. Just thinking of it gave her tingles. She could always repay Dette when she sold her house in the spring. "Okay," she said.

Dette punched the air with such gusto Annie was grateful she was not in her friend's immediate vicinity.

Dette's apparent glee proved infectious and with an optimistic enthusiasm, she led Dette upstairs to show her the hole she had made in the carpet.

CHAPTER NINE

Annie had jitters, butterflies, heart palpitations, and every other metaphor or cliché for anxiety. This would be her first league hockey game in nearly four years.

As she had played competitive hockey most of her life, just the two words "league game" filled her head with the ghosts of games past – ties, shoot-outs, playoffs, and even tryouts. Looking around the room, she knew she was one of the oldest (if not *the* oldest) player in the room. They all looked so young, so fit.

Dette had introduced everyone to Annie, and she could remember hardly any of their names, which made her feel even older.

Annie pulled on the jersey Dette had given her. In her haste, it got hooked on her shoulder pads. She stood up to try to wriggle into it. She got stuck and stood there a moment feeling like a monkey with dislocated shoulders. The girl next to her, a woman really, but she looked young enough to be Annie's daughter, reached over and yanked Annie's jersey into place.

"Thanks," Annie said, both grateful and embarrassed.

She swallowed another wave of nervousness. She had managed to hold her own with the men; surely she could keep up with some of these women.

During the warm-up, she eyed the opposition with increasing trepidation. The other team looked young and big, and most were very good skaters.

Annie allowed herself a sigh. What was the worst that could happen? She could look like a pylon and be asked to leave the team. At least she was giving it a try.

She pushed away her anxiety with the conviction to work as hard as she could and enjoy what could be her last league game.

The coach, the husband of one of the ladies, put Annie on right wing with Dette on the left. George was at centre. Annie remembered that name only because it was unusual, short for Georgette, Dette had said. They were to be the third line out. The wait allowed Annie's nervousness to resurface in spite of her resolve against it.

When it came time for Annie's line to go out, she automatically did what she had done in games past, hop over the boards. Only this time she got caught up on someone's stick and ended up going ass over teakettle.

Giggles ensued, mixed with queries as to her well-being and a sincere apology from the girl who had helped Annie with her jersey.

George extended a hand to help Annie up, but she did not need nor want the hand and waved it off. She got to her feet and skated to the face-off circle as confidently as she could.

Great first impression, Annie thought, and worried that superstition claimed such events often came in threes.

Just before the referee dropped the puck, she saw Jonathan Dooley in the stands and inwardly cringed. He must have seen her second embarrassment. Too late she saw the puck slide past her. In her distraction she had missed the face-off.

And that would make number three, she thought.

As she skated hard after the puck carrier, she wondered how many more faux pas she would accumulate before this game was over. A new record for sure.

It took three shifts for Annie to get used to the fast pace. But she did manage to steal the puck a couple of times and had a shot on net before the end of the period.

During the second period, hockey did its usual magic and her world became the game at hand. Each time she managed to intercept a pass or back-checked to prevent a shot on their goalie, it inspired her to do more.

At the end of the second period, the game was tied one-one. The coach gathered them all to the bench.

"Good work," he said. "This team is at the top of the standings and we are holding our own, but I'd like to change things up a bit."

He looked at Annie. "You're the hardest worker out there. I'd like you to play center between Jen and Dette."

Annie loved playing center, but it involved a lot more skating than the wing position did. She was grateful for the short shifts as each time she returned to the bench she was gasping for air. Her upper body had never been strong and the best she could do at each face-off was a draw.

With five minutes left in the game, Annie's line skated onto the ice with the face-off in their end. She swung at the dropped puck but missed it entirely and the other center passed it right back to her defenseman. That player wound up and her slap shot sent the puck flying past Annie's ear.

Their goalie stopped the puck, but it bounced off her chest right onto the stick of the opposition's center.

Annie stretched out to stop the shot, but it was too late. The puck was in the net.

The coach put the next line out. No one said anything, but Annie felt responsible even though she knew no one player should feel responsible for a goal. She had often said such to other teammates to lessen their guilt after a goal against them. But taking one's own advice was always harder than giving it.

With only thirty seconds left in the game and with the face-off in the opposing end, the coach pulled their goalie and put out George's line. He told Dette to go out on defense, and, to Annie's surprise, he put her out as the extra skater.

For the face-off, Annie stood at the top of the circle, between Dette and the net.

George won the draw cleanly back to Dette. Annie turned to face the net in anticipation of a rebound. Then she felt the puck bounce off her left shoulder pad.

Damn it! She had just blocked Dette's hard shot! Frustrated, she reached for the puck and dumped it towards the net.

Miraculously, it made it past a crowd of skates, including the goalie's. Annie looked at the clock. She had tied the game with just seven seconds left.

Elation pulsed through her.

"Way to go, Antsy!" Dette thumped Annie on the shoulder with such gusto that Annie nearly fell over.

Annie wanted to rebut with the fact that if she hadn't blocked Dette's great shot in the first place, Dette would have no doubt scored but cheers and additional thumps on her back didn't allow her to utter a word.

In the dressing room, Annie continued to enjoy the game's after-glow, something she had not felt in a long time. Even a twinge of guilt at feeling so good with Gil gone didn't last long.

"I'm glad you weren't injured when I made you fall over the boards," the girl to her left said. "Sorry about that."

"No worries, Jen," Annie answered, praying she had the name right. Jen was one of the younger ones and Annie had seen her arrive with a young man holding the hand of a toddler.

"You are really good," Jen added. "How long have you been playing?"

"More than thirty-five years," Annie answered. "Long enough to know better. How about you?" she asked.

"About a year and a half ago I started playing to try to lose the baby weight."

"Oh man, you are doing so well." Worried Jen would think she was talking about the weight loss and not the hockey, Annie quickly added, "You look like you've been playing hockey a lot longer than that."

Jen smiled shyly. "Thanks. I really enjoy it. And I think Billy is kinda proud of the fact his wife plays hockey."

Annie darted into the bathroom to change her sweat-dampened underwear. She caught her image in the mirror. Her short dark hair was plastered to her scalp, rounding out her reddened features that, even in this dim light, revealed too many wrinkles. More than when she moved here, she thought. But her eyes had a light in them. Endorphins from the exertion, perhaps.

Thoughts of a certain doctor may have also helped. Jonathan had probably witnessed her mistakes. Hopefully he had stayed to see her goal.

"Hurry up, Antsy," Dette said the moment Annie exited the bathroom. "I told Gran I'd be home in time to watch wrestling with her."

As they neared the rink entrance, Annie heard someone behind her say, "Nice goal." Before she turned around, her heart had begun a step dance.

Jonathan's eyes soon found hers. "How about I treat you ladies to some well-deserved cholesterol?"

"I can't but Antsy can," Dette said.

Annie turned to her friend and waved her keys. "I drove, remember?" She swung back to Jonathan. "Can I drop her off, first?" she asked, trying to mask the eagerness bursting within her.

"No need," Dette said, grabbing Annie's keys. "I'll drive your car home and bring it back tomorrow."

Dette extracted the house key from Annie's key chain and handed it back. "Go with him, Antsy. He's harmless enough, aren't you, Doc? Besides . . ." She stepped close to Jonathan. She was nearly as tall as he and the hockey bag widened her frame considerably. "If he harms either a physical or emotional hair on that wee head of yours, he'll be eating a hockey stick sandwich that'll keep him removing splinters from what is left of his molars for years. And he understands this, don't you, Doc?"

Jonathan laughed hard. "That I do." He held the door open for Dette. "Ladies first," he said, his eyes wrinkled with suppressed laughter.

As Annie passed him, he grabbed her hockey bag, hoisted it over his shoulder, and steered her by the elbow towards a large SUV. Even through her padded winter jacket she could feel the warmth of his hand.

While he threw her bag and stick into the back, she slipped into the passenger seat and tried to calm the thrill animating her every cell. It's just the high from the hockey game, she tried to tell herself.

Jonathan slid into the driver's seat and with him so close, all she could think about was when and if he was going to kiss her. He smoothly backed the vehicle out of the parking spot and headed towards the exit.

"Where do you want to go?" he asked, keeping his eyes on the street ahead.

Her stomach rumbled. "You did promise me cholesterol and I haven't had a burger in ages." A part of her worried that the doctor in him might look down on her fondness for junk food. Best he learn her bad points quickly, she thought. This could be a good opportunity for her to discover other reasons why she should not let this thing progress further. Or why she should.

His grin, however, was full of approval. "A&W okay?"

"Absolutely."

As he drove into the A&W parking lot, the idea came to her to suggest they get take-out and eat at her place, but before she could say anything, he had parked and turned off the engine.

Inside, he stood behind her while they waited in line and when he placed a warm hand on her shoulder, she had to resist an urge to lean back against him. Too soon the path cleared to the counter.

She ordered a Teen Burger meal with a root beer and was inwardly pleased when he ordered the same. She was about to nix the fries, but the ones handed to the fellow in the other line smelled terrific and it had been so long since she had them that she decided to keep quiet.

Her stomach rumbled again in anticipation and she was grateful the food was quickly served. Soon they sat down with their meals in front of them.

He took a couple of bites of his burger before he said "Mmm, this is so good it's got to be really bad for us."

She nodded and reached for a fry. It practically melted in her mouth, leaving a salty aftertaste that demanded more, followed by a sip of root beer chilled to perfection by its frosted glass.

A dollop of mustard lingered at the corner of his mouth. As if her hand had a life of its own, it reached across the table to dab at it with her napkin. He froze and this forced her to do the same. She jerked her arm back to her half of the table.

His gentle thanks cut off her apology. He smiled at her, the light in his eyes turning the soft brown into more of a golden hazel.

Shit. Sparks. Huge, hot sparks. She focused on her fries. "I'm going to eat every last one of these," she said.

Instead of the expected criticism he had totally denied her to this point, he asked, "Want one of my Lipitor pills?"

She laughed. "No thanks, though, God knows, I probably need it. I guess I should get my cholesterol checked. Though I probably won't be here long enough to need a family doctor."

"Hellooooo," he said. "You've already seen a good doctor."

"Yeah, right, I'd love to see you for a physical." Oh god, she thought. Did I really say that? Her cheeks burned while he laughed. She took a long, deep breath, hoping the extra oxygen would stabilize her thoughts.

He had stopped laughing, but his eyes hadn't. "I was thinking of my daughter. I'm sure I could convince her to accept you as a regular."

Annie blushed anew at the memory of her most recent visit to the clinic and she pretended to study her fries.

When he spoke again, his tone had turned sober. "I didn't know your move here was only temporary."

She nodded. "The plan is to fix the house up, then sell it and move back to Toronto."

He finished his root beer. "Great choice for dinner," he said, though his eyes, when they again found hers, were a darker shade.

A sliver of optimism caused her to wonder if he was sad at the thought of her leaving.

Although she had finished her burger, half of the fries remained. She put them back onto the tray. "I'm sorry, I lied about eating all of them. I'm full. Thanks for supper."

His gaze penetrated hers when he said, "You're welcome. I guess I should take you home now."

The sky had begun to spit a cold rain that threatened to turn to sleet and he hurriedly opened the passenger door for her. Annie pushed aside a wave of disappointment that he hadn't taken this opportunity to kiss her.

The drive home was too short. She joined him at the back of his vehicle while he hauled out her hockey bag and stick. The raised rear door created a bit of shelter from the frozen pellets. When he pulled her hockey bag over his shoulder and handed over her hockey stick, she figured he had decided not to kiss her.

But he pushed the bag behind his back and with his free arm he pulled her close. He stooped a little so his head cleared the raised door and she didn't have to stand on her toes. This kiss was long, deep and sent a tingling need through her.

Then he shut the door, took her hand, and together they ran to the porch. Impatience now ruled and Annie had to go through three pockets to find the slim house key. Then it snagged on a thread. She yanked it free, and after a long minute of fumbling, managed to unlock the door. She looked up and expected to find him laughing at her.

But instead his brow was furrowed and he looked . . . she searched for the word and found it: uncomfortable. He looked downright uncomfortable.

But she asked anyway, though she already knew the answer. "Do you want to come in?"

"Uh . . . no . . . I'd . . . uh . . . I'd better get going." He looked as if he was about to say more, but instead, he dropped her hockey bag and jogged back to his vehicle.

She waited until the sound of his departing car faded.

All that remained was the ping of frozen rain on the roof of the veranda.

What just happened? He had seemed so attentive, so interested. And that kiss. She could have read volumes into that kiss. She looked around the porch, searching for an answer, then thought she found one.

Even in the long shadows cast by the street lamp, she could make out the dilapidated state of the porch, which she was certain, was reflected in the rest of the house.

Yep, he probably realized that she was a struggling single female. Alhough a wiser part of her brain told her that this was grasping at a straw in a huge haystack, she could think of no other reason for his behaviour.

Better sooner than later, she decided. She was on the downhill side of fifty, for Pete's sake. Romance should be off the books. Not needed. Not wanted. The falsehood in these last words hit her the moment she stepped inside and the dreaded heaviness greeted her once more.

It'll be all right.

Too weary to argue with imagined whispers, she emptied her equipment out to dry in the back porch, then, picking up a still sleeping Temp off the couch, she headed for the stairs. Hopefully, fatigue from hockey would grant her easy access to the unconscious realm where she wouldn't have to deal with anything, past or present.

CHAPTER TEN

"And then?" Dette leaned nearly halfway across the small table.

Annie paused to sip her tea. "And then . . . he left."

"You twit! You didn't invite him in?"

"I did. He looked very uncomfortable and left without so much as a handshake." She hoped she sounded nonplussed.

Dette shrugged. "Maybe he's shy."

He hadn't kissed like someone who was shy, Annie thought. "Maybe he took one look at this place and decided not to get involved with a destitute widow."

"That's bonkers, Annie. Give the guy a chance."

Gran's words returned to Annie: *Be patient with him.* Could she have meant Jonathan? What else had Gran said? She pulled at the memory. Oh yes. *He's sensitive.*

Before Annie could ponder this further, Dette went on. "I wouldn't write him off just yet. Hey, there's a co-ed tournament in Baddeck next Saturday. You going?"

Annie appreciated Dette's obvious change of topic. "I doubt it."

"Ooh, don't let Dr. Shy keep you from playing some

good hockey. Thing is, they're only taking fifteen skaters, so you'd better speak up at next week's shinny. Oh fuck! Is that the tenth?" She looked at the calendar next to the stove. "Shit a brick, it is. I told Jimmy I'd work that night for him. You should go, though. It's a fast game, as good as a league game. It'd be good for you, though you played well enough last night." She grinned. "Although you could use some practice hopping over the boards."

Annie stuck her tongue out. Dette always managed to bring out Annie's inner child.

Dette stood and stretched. "Well, let's get back to the carpet stripping."

They'd found a bit of a treasure beneath the carpets: nearly pristine wood floors that, according to Dette, would need just a bit of sanding and Verathane to make them look like new.

Just as Annie was about to follow Dette up the stairs, a solid knock on the front door startled her. The hope that Jonathan had come to explain his quick departure flitted through Annie's head before she quickly shoved it onto the fantasy shelf. Still, she hurried to the door and flung it open.

It was not Jonathan who stood there, but another man. One she did not recognize. He appeared to be in his mid-forties and wore an expensive-looking coat over what looked to be an equally expensive suit.

"Annie Terrell?" he asked.

"Yes?"

"I'm Dennis MacPhee, your aunt's lawyer."

"Oh, yes." She stepped back and gestured for him to come inside, well aware of her faded jeans and sweater. Worry niggled into her brain. Had this man discovered a clause in Jessie's will that would nullify any claim Annie had on the house? Her mouth became so dry that she couldn't speak.

It will be all right.

Annie hoped the whisper would for once prove correct and offered the man a seat on the sofa.

He declined, most likely because he had noticed the film of dust on everything, compliments of old carpet remnants being bounced down the stairs and lugged through the house to the back door. Then he sneezed. And sneezed again, this time more violently.

"I'm so sorry," Annie said. "We've been ripping up carpets."

"Denny?" Dette stood at the bottom of the stairs. "Wee Denny MacPhee?"

His eyebrows formed a frown above watering eyes. "Yes?"

"Hah! I'm Dette! Sydney Academy, graduate of '75. And this is Annie MacInnis, now Terrell. We tried out for the boy's varsity hockey team, remember?"

His eyes widened then squeezed tightly shut before he let loose with another sneeze, one that shook his entire body. Over a silk handkerchief, he peered from Annie to Dette. "Do you have a . . . cat!" He jumped back as Temp tried to wrap herself around one of his legs.

He backed against the door and Annie scooped up a purring Temp who was obviously intent on convincing the poor fellow that she was not really the cause of his sneezing.

Annie handed Temp over to Dette. "Take her out to the kitchen, will you?"

"Of course." Dette cradled Temp like a baby and started rubbing the feline's exposed belly on the way to the kitchen.

Annie turned back to Dennis just in time to see him sneeze so violently into his hanky that she feared for his brains. "Sorry about that."

He waved off her apology and reached inside his coat.

He withdrew a thin white envelope and handed it to her. "I'm not supposed to give you this until the New Year." His voice had thickened and his words were rounded. He opened the door and stood in the doorway, letting in unwelcome winter cold, but Annie didn't have the heart to deny him fresh air.

He blew his nose, but his words still came out syrupy. "I'm taking my kids skiing in Banff over Christmas and I won't be back until the sixth of January, so I thought I'd drop it off early."

She looked at the envelope. "Open Jan 1st" was hand-printed on the outside. "What is it?"

He blew his nose again. "It's from your aunt. She was really adamant about the exact date you get this and although she's not here to fire me . . ." He sneezed and stepped further back onto the porch. "Please wait to open it in the New Year." He handed her a card. "Call me after January six if you have any questions."

Annie shut the door behind his retreating figure and stared at the envelope a moment before parking it on the mantel beside the clock. She then joined Dette in the kitchen who was still holding a purring Temp.

"Who would've thunk," Dette said. "Wee Denny aging into a hunk."

"Aren't you supposed to be gay?"

Dette snorted. "That doesn't stop me from admiring a fine specimen, especially when I'm on the lookout for a certain single friend of mine. Maybe all Dr. Shy needs is a little com-pe-ti-tion." She swung her hips in rhythm with each syllable.

Annie expelled air in disgust. "Denny's married, with children."

"I heard he's divorced. And he's a lot cuter than Jonathan."

"And allergic to cats, as well as being a lot younger."

Dette shook her head like a child refusing medicine. "Nope. He was just a year behind us in school. At our age that's nothin'. Besides, I saw him checking you out."

Annie blew out a sigh and put on the kettle for another cup of tea, a brew she hardly drank before coming back to Cape Breton.

"What'd he want anyway?" Dette said.

"He left me a note from Aunt Jessie that I'm not supposed to open until the New Year. Typical of Jessie, bossy even from beyond the grave."

Dette's eyebrows rose, her right one faster than her left. "Hmmm, it appears you are haunted, after all."

* * * *

Annie could not help but smile as she stepped off the ice. It had been a good shinny. Not only had her side won, but she had managed to take the puck from Jonathan at least three times. At one face-off he'd grinned widely at her, as though she weren't a carrier of the bubonic plague after all.

"Annie!" Carla called to her from across the dressing room. "Bob wants to know if he can put you down for the tournament in Baddeck on Saturday. They need one more female player to meet their quota."

When Annie hesitated, Dette piped up. "I gotta work but you really should go, Antsy. You've no reason not to. Besides, there won't be any hockey after that until the New Year."

It was this last fact that convinced Annie. She nodded at Carla. "Okay, put me down."

Annie stepped outside into a particularly biting wind.

She pulled the hood of her jacket up, lowered her head to keep it in place and jogged towards her Subaru, her hockey bag bouncing roughly against her back.

Jonathan leaned against her car, obviously waiting for her. Even with his posture hunched against the chill wind and his head covered by a toque, a thread of attraction tickled her. Maybe he is shy, she thought. Or, maybe he changed his mind about her. Better he didn't, she tried to tell herself, but her body was not listening.

"Good game," he said, his smile definitely void of any of the discomfort he experienced the previous Friday. "You going to the tournament in Baddeck on Saturday?"

"I am." She opened the rear door and threw her bag inside and tried to keep both her voice and movements non-committal, non-emotional, and certainly not eager.

"Want to travel together?" he asked. When she hesitated, he quickly added, "I live in Winsome Heights. It's off Big Bras D'Or Lake and right on the way to Baddeck. I figured you could drive to my place, then we could travel the rest of the way together."

No, no, no, said her mind. Yes, yes, yes, countered her heart. She must have nodded as he handed her a folded piece of paper. "Here are the directions to my place. We should leave around nine."

When she took it from him, his eyes crinkled above a smile that pulled at her. If he were to lean down to kiss her, she knew she would not stop him.

But after a glance over her shoulder, he backed away. "See you Saturday," he said and then nodded to an approaching Dette before jogging through the wind to his vehicle.

Annie pulled her eyes away from Jonathan's retreating form. "You coming over this aft?" she asked Dette.

"No, that's what I wanted to tell ya," Dette said. "I'd better see to Gran. She's got the sniffles again. What's up with the good doctor?"

"We're going to drive to Baddeck together."

"Awesome, Antsy. I told ya to be patient." She shivered. "Christ, that wind is fucking cold."

Annie nodded. "Tell Gran I said hi," she said before diving into her car, feeling energized from anticipation that was not at all related to hockey.

CHAPTER ELEVEN

The moment they entered the Victoria Highland Civic Centre in Baddeck, Annie felt something was not quite right.

Jonathan held the entrance door open for her go ahead of him. To reach their dressing room they had to pass by the boards and glass surrounding the ice.

Her odd feeling was validated when a puck whizzed along the glass at the level of her head. She realized it came from a wrist shot by a man young enough to be her son.

She stopped and turned back to Jonathan. "Uh, I thought this tournament was a fund-raiser, like, for fun?"

Jonathan studied the game a moment before he answered. "Maybe we should have asked if there were any restrictions on age or skill. Some of these guys look awfully fast."

Jonathan had told her earlier that he wouldn't be able to play in the final game on Sunday as he was scheduled to fly to Vancouver in the afternoon. But by the looks of the game in front of her, Annie doubted their team would even qualify for the final game anyway.

This was the first time Annie had to share a dressing room with men, although it didn't seem to bother the other two women: Carla from the Dames and another girl, Stephanie, who looked to be at least twenty years younger.

Gerry, the organizer, made up the lines and put one woman on each line. They put Annie on wing with Jonathan as the centre and someone named Joe on the other wing.

Just after the game started, Jonathan turned to her and said, "Just try not to get hurt."

Annie nodded and figured she would have to skate her butt off just to stay out of everyone's way.

Their turn came. Annie tried to swallow away her nervousness as she skated to the face-off circle in the opposing end.

Jonathan winked at her, then focused on the ref's hand. He won the draw and sent the puck right to Annie.

Perhaps the defenseman opposite Annie didn't expect an old lady like her to actually be able to corral the pass, or maybe he was just being nice, but the moment the puck met the tape on her stick, she threw it at the net.

The goalie grabbed for it, juggled it, and Jonathan tapped it out of the air into the net.

Her team cheered and she couldn't help but smile.

But as hard as she skated and as focused as she tried to be, all she could do was try to keep up to the play and watch her man in their end. Having to go full out every second soon wore on her and she was grateful they had three lines.

They ended up losing 7-3, but Annie came off the ice with a nice post-game high. She had made few mistakes and at least hadn't felt like an albatross around the team's neck. Most importantly, she hadn't gotten hurt.

Their next game was just two hours later, too soon
for stiffness or fatigue to set in so everyone still played
with a lot of energy. They lost 3-1 and Annie's tired body
made her grateful she didn't have to play in the final the
next day. She would be sore enough and besides, she
wouldn't have wanted to drive back to Baddeck alone.

Someone mentioned it was snowing outside, so they
hurriedly changed and headed out.

Living in downtown Toronto had limited Annie's
winter driving experience so she was anxious to get the
trip over with and was grateful Jonathan didn't suggest
they stop to eat along the way.

The thickening snow reduced visibility. Jonathan had
offered to take his vehicle, but no, she had to act like
Miss Independent. Miss Strong. Miss Stupid, she thought
as she blinked past the windshield wipers.

The ride to the rink in Baddeck, uncomplicated by bad
weather, had consisted of light banter and hockey talk.
The ride home proved much quieter, with both of them
focused on the road. She worried Jonathan was wishing
he was driving instead of her.

She felt his eyes on her, but, as much as she wanted to
look at him, she figured she'd better keep her gaze glued
to the road ahead.

"You played well," he said at length, probably to break
up the tense silence. "Nice assist," he added in a voice so
smooth Annie thought that maybe he wasn't so nervous
about her driving after all.

"Nice goal," she countered. "And you won that draw
or we wouldn't have scored." She sighed. "That pace was
much too fast for me, though."

"Don't sell yourself short. We held our own and most
of the players were a lot younger than us."

"How old are you, anyway?" Annie asked in an effort
to keep the conversation going.

"Nearly four years older than you."

She risked a quick glance at him. "How do you . . . oh yeah, the medical clinic."

"Yeah, I kinda had to look at your file before I examined you."

His words prompted an image of him examining more than her knee and Annie quickly shoved that thought aside.

"I would have pegged you as being in your early forties," he added.

"Hardly," Annie said.

"I'm a doctor. I know a lot of women over fifty who would prove my point."

The wind picked up and reduced visibility even more, which allowed Annie a reasonable excuse for not responding. They weren't too far from his place now, thank goodness.

After turning onto the road to Jonathan's subdivision and into the shelter of the tall trees, the view improved slightly. The homes here were widely spaced and with the light traffic the road was a blanket of white.

As they neared his cul de sac new worries compounded the existing ones: how huge and expensive his house had looked when she picked him up. Would he kiss her when they got back there? Would he ask her to stay and wait out the bad weather?

She felt as rattled as she had ever been since coming home to Cape Breton, so why wasn't her whisper telling her it would be all right?

Jonathan's calm voice pierced her worry. "Take the next left," he said.

She was grateful for the instruction, as nightfall had changed the landscape she had navigated earlier. She made the turn and the white expanse of Big Bras d'Or Lake on her right meant Jonathan's driveway was the very next one.

She pulled into a long drive that curved behind giant spruce trees. As she came to a stop in front of the double garage, the outside lights came on and bathed the inside of her vehicle. She ignored his eyes and peered through her side window. The falling snow looked less ominous now so she didn't turn off the engine. She would wait for him to get out, take his gear from the back, and then she would leave.

But instead of saying goodbye, getting out, or anything that would appease her inner battle, he just waited silently, forcing her to look at him.

"You shouldn't drive back to Sydney in this weather," he said.

She pulled away from his gaze and pretended to study the skies again. "It isn't so bad. I'll take my time."

"Variably cloudy, they'd said, so it shouldn't last long. Why not come in and let me cook us some supper? By the time we eat, it'll probably have stopped."

Without waiting for an answer he got out, came around to her side, and opened her door. "Please. I promise to behave myself."

I'd rather you wouldn't, she thought as she got out. He pulled his bag out of the back and led her up the steps to the front door.

He unlocked the door and waited for her to enter ahead of him. The moment she stepped inside the foyer, the difference in their financial situations became painfully evident.

Marble tiles gleamed beneath a large chandelier. He flicked a switch to reveal a room before them that was larger than the entire ground floor of her house.

To her left stood a granite-topped island that separated the ultra-modern kitchen from the living room where a leather sofa faced a large flat-screen television. A love seat parked at an angle in front of a gas fireplace. The whole back wall consisted of a floor-to-ceiling window beyond which the blackness of night hid what was probably a spectacular view of the lake.

"This is absolutely gorgeous," she said.

"I had a lot of help with the design. Hungry?" He headed for the refrigerator. The question as to who gave him the help niggled at Annie but she pushed it aside.

"Are you always this tidy?" she said to his back as he stooped to search the freezer drawer at the bottom of the fridge. She allowed herself a good look at a backside tightened by skating.

He waved off her words. "Nope. It's only this clean because I have a lady come in and she was here yesterday. Aha!" He pulled a package out and waved it at her. "Salmon?" His eyes were bright, eager, and almost child-like in their search for her approval.

She laughed, relishing her lightened mood, though she did try to reign in the burgeoning anticipation. "You don't have to go to any bother. A sandwich will do."

"No bother," he said as he approached her.

She knew what was coming and she didn't back away. His kiss was soft, long, and damn it, her knees *did* feel weak. And, oh Christ, she had just played hockey and probably smelled like it. She pulled back, though that was the last thing she felt like doing.

"I really need a shower," she said, alarmed that her words came out in a husky whisper. Oh my God, I'm a walking cliché.

He stepped back. "I do too, and I did promise to behave myself. Let me show you the guest bathroom." He set the frozen fish on the counter, took her hand and led her up the open staircase nestled at the back of the room, flicking on lights as they went.

His hand was warm and gentle and she had no

intention of letting go until he did. He led her into a large bathroom. Like the downstairs, everything was modern and expensive. He opened a built-in cabinet to reveal a stack of thick towels, all white.

"There should be shampoo in the shower stall." He pointed to a wall of glass blocks. "If you need anything else, just holler."

He left her alone in a dream-like state that she could only describe as euphoric. His obvious acceptance of her financial state had blown away the storm riding within her and left in its wake a burning expectation. Get a grip, girl, she told herself. Don't go hoping for something that you really don't want to happen.

But she did allow herself to enjoy the moment. She stripped and stepped behind the glass wall into a large shower with a nozzle that adjusted in more directions than she would have thought possible.

The hot water washed away the hockey sweat and enhanced the high wave on which she was riding. She told herself a portion of her mood was a result of lingering endorphins from the hockey. Where the rest was coming from, she refused to think about.

As she toweled down, she gave her body a cursory assessment. She had not aged too badly, thanks to her addiction to physical activity. But there were a few spots, particularly around her waist that could use more toning. When she wiped the steam off the mirror, the bright light revealed her proliferating facial wrinkles.

She opened a few drawers and discovered a tube of sunscreen that was also a moisturizer, so she borrowed a glob of that. Further exploration rewarded her with hair gel. She wondered who owned these female products, as his daughter was married with children and did not reside here. But she refused to let this cloud her thoughts or stop her from using the bit of make-up she found in the lower drawer.

She applied eyeliner and darkened her thinning brows, donned her underwear and began another search for a hair dryer. When none could be found, she wrapped the bath towel around her, and opened the door. The sound of silverware being jostled came from the kitchen.

"Jonathan?" she called.

There was no response, so she raised her voice and called again.

Footsteps stopped at the bottom of the stairs. "Yes?"

"Do you have a hairdryer I could borrow?"

She hastily closed the door as he thundered up the stairs. A second later there was a timid knock. She stood behind the door and opened it only a few inches. A small black hair dryer appeared in the opening.

"Sorry, this is all I have."

She took it, closed the door, and hollered, "Thank-you."

The fact that it was obviously a man's hair dryer rendered her earlier worry moot, as another female regularly inhabiting the premises would surely need a more versatile one. She dropped the towel but before she could turn the dryer on there was another timid knock. Her chicken feathers grew even larger and she spoke through the closed door. "Yes?"

"Uh . . I've got an outfit of my daughter's, er," he sounded as nervous as she felt. "It's probably too big for you. Anyhow, I'll leave it here . . . by the door . . . if you want."

Before she could thank him heavy footsteps headed back down the stairs. She opened the door to find folded on the floor a black t-shirt and what looked like yoga pants. The fitted t-shirt was the perfect size. The pants were snug about her waist but the legs were too long and had to be rolled up.

She stood back to allow the mirror to show as much of her body as possible. Not bad, she thought, thanks to the slimming properties of the color, especially if she sucked in her gut.

She then noticed her hair. Shit, it had started to kink and without a brush she had no hope of trying to style it. She attempted to finger-style as she dried her hair, and soon pieces began to stick up in the wrong places. She had not had her haircut since leaving Toronto and it was outgrowing what shape it had.

She sighed at her image. Horrible hair. Straight figure. Not a siren, that was for sure.

The savory aroma of baked salmon greeted her at the head of the stairs. When she reached the bottom she found Jonathan bent over the stove. His hair was still slightly damp; his own shower had obviously been quicker than hers. When he straightened up his broad shoulders outflanked his hips and caused a twitter in her stomach.

Settle down, girl, she told herself.

He motioned to the table, which was set for two, with a large, single white candle adorning the middle. He said little, and moved quickly as he arranged a salad and the salmon onto the plates, a frown of concentration on his features.

But when he sat down across from her, the frown was erased by a warm, though brief grin. He raised his glass of wine. "I assumed white was okay?"

She took a sip. "Pinot Grigio?"

His grin was more brilliant and lasted longer this time. "Very good."

The plate in front of her looked appetizing as well as healthy. "Very nice," she said. "A man who cooks."

"This isn't much."He grimaced slightly which she found cute as well.

The wine was crisp, cold, and its mellowing effect immediate. She cautioned herself to sip slowly in the event the weather cleared up enough for her to drive home.

The tender salmon melted upon her palate. She gave in to her hunger and finished her plate in a matter of minutes. She looked up, dismayed to see him still working on his.

"There's more." He made a motion to get up but she waved him back down.

"No, thanks, that was plenty. I was so hungry, I just wolfed it down." She raised her glass. "Kudos to the chef."

"No wonder you were hungry." He glanced at his watch. "Eight-thirty-five. A rather late meal and after two games of hockey, too." He paused to study her and his eyes made her want to leap over the table at him.

Instead she leapt for distraction. "Do you have other children?"

He nodded. "My son lives in Vancouver." He hesitated a moment. "We're going to spend Christmas at his place." Another hesitation. "I won't be back until after the New Year."

On one level, Annie was disappointed that she wouldn't see him for more than two weeks. On another she was relieved that she wouldn't have to worry about seeing him during the dreaded holiday season. Although spending time with Gran and Dette would ease things, she would be relieved when the New Year began.

As if he had read her thoughts, he asked, "When did you lose your husband?"

"Two years ago last April." His question emboldened her to ask, "And your wife?"

"It's been almost ten years. Sometimes it seems a lot longer. Then sometimes it feels like yesterday."

The previous niggle about a female on the premises blossomed into a noggle. Surely he had dated since then. A man this good-looking could not have remained alone for long. She studied him and there was nothing, absolutely nothing but kindness and goodness leaking from his soul.

After a moment, he stood, walked to her end of the table, removed his glasses and bent down to kiss her. Though she was still sitting, her knees quivered.

He pulled away, and asked, "May I take your plate, madam?"

You can take more than that, she thought. She got up and helped him clear the table.

At the dishwasher, he surprised her by asking, "Do you believe in ghosts?" His face was so serious that she took a moment to compose her answer.

"No." She was certain the whispers she heard were only symptoms of a coping mechanism she had created as a child. "If there were, I'm sure I would have seen some by now. There's been a lot of deaths, Gil's being the most painful. My parents passed so suddenly, I never got to say goodbye." Or reconcile with. "But I honestly think that was easier. With Gil, it was like saying good-bye for months and that was hard. You must have gone through something similar."

He shook his head. "We thought she had the cancer beaten. Then, right after she finished the chemo, she got this cold. She was so weak that the pneumonia took her in a day."

The sadness in his voice hung in the room. "The kids were away at university so they never got to say goodbye. I didn't either, for that matter. There had been a multi-vehicle accident on the Edmonton Trail and I was in emergency downstairs. They called me when she went into respiratory arrest but by the time I got there it was too late." He looked away and his eyes narrowed. "I often wish I could have been with her when she went."

A blast of wind shook the window over the sink.

He stepped up to the French doors and switched on an outside light. "You won't be going anywhere soon."

Through the glass all Annie could see was a pulsing blizzard. In the brief pauses between gusts of wind, she could almost make out the outline of a huge deck, but they passed so quickly she wondered if her brain was conjuring up what she suspected to be there. Anticipation and fear of spending the night volleyed in her head.

"So much for a passing squall. What time are you supposed to fly out tomorrow?" she asked.

"Not until the afternoon, though this storm is sure to back the flights up." He turned and smiled at her. "But I'm not going to worry about that now."

He reached past her to close the dishwasher door, his proximity stirring Annie once more. She wanted him to kiss her and to hide this she asked, "What about you? Do you believe in ghosts?"

His features froze for a moment. "Uh, yeah, I guess. I think that what we can see isn't necessarily all there is."

Fascinated that a man of science would think this, Annie leaned towards him. "Have you ever seen one?"

He hesitated so long that Annie thought he was about to answer in the affirmative, but he didn't. "No . . . no, I haven't."

"Do you believe in God?" Annie asked, surprised by her own brashness.

"Yes," he said. "Yes I do. You?"

"No," Annie said. "My parents attended church religiously, pardon the pun. But I am a true-blue atheist. There is too much pain in the world for a so-called benevolent, all-knowing deity to exist. Do I sound cynical?"

"Not really," he said softly. "You sound like someone who's been through a lot."

Not wanting to sound pathetic, she countered, "I've done all right. The twenty-six years I spent with Gil were, until that last two, terrific. I got to do what I wanted to do."

"Which was what?" he interrupted.

"Write. Play hockey." She smiled. She should be grateful she had it so good for so long.

His eyebrows arched. "What do you write?"

"Fiction. I haven't written a thing since Gil took sick. The only thing I had published was a collection of short stories." She didn't add her book had received critical acclaim, and that, before Gil's diagnosis, she had considered applying for a writer-in-residence position at the University of Toronto.

She looked up to see his eyes locked onto hers once more.

A thrill ran through her when he removed his glasses and leaned down. This time his arm snaked around her waist and pulled her against him. She put her arms on his shoulders and their kiss deepened. When they finished kissing, she wanted him to hold her forever.

But he let go and waved at the window. "You really can't head out in this." He looked at her intently, as if gauging her reaction, which she tried desperately to hide.

"I love listening to storms," she said. "Just give me another glass of wine and turn on that fireplace. Between it and the storm, I will be well entertained." With any luck, she would fall asleep and awaken in the morning, having done nothing she would regret.

"Well, I guess I could let you do that while I go pack."

"You haven't packed yet?"

He laughed. "No. Typical guy, eh?" He pulled out a fresh wine glass and filled it nearly to the rim. "If this doesn't hold you, there is another chilled bottle in the fridge."

She took it from him, and let her fingers slide over his. "Are you trying to ply me with alcohol?"

He leaned back a little. "No."

"That's too bad." The words came out before she could swallow them, but to her relief he laughed. "Seriously," she said in what she hoped was a normal voice. "Go pack."

On the way past the fireplace, he flipped a switch that turned on the gas and then headed up the stairs.

Annie settled onto the leather love seat and sipped the wine. She knew she should take it slow as the brew could dissolve what control she had left. She focused on the sound of the storm and the accompanying dance of the flames.

* * * *

A gentle hand on her arm startled her.

"Sorry . . . you fell asleep."

The now-empty wine glass sat beside her on an end table. It and the wind's serenade had lulled her to sleep.

"I've made up a bed for you in one of the spare bedrooms," he said.

So, no invite to the master, she thought, both relieved and disappointed. "It's still storming?"

"It is. And even if it wasn't I wouldn't let you drive home tonight anyway." He pointed to her empty glass.

She let him guide her up the stairs, his hand warm on the small of her back. She allowed herself a brief fantasy as to where she would like that hand to go.

The room was next to the bathroom she had showered in earlier. The bed, though soft and welcoming, looked empty, unused. The wind was louder here as it fought with the nearby trees.

He turned her around and kissed her. She leaned against him and was rewarded with his hands, one resting on her shoulder and the other cupping her opposite shoulder blade.

As they pulled apart, they sighed in unison and this made them both giggle.

"You know, I hate storms," he said.

She poked him playfully. "Oh, are you scared?"

"No . . . well, sort of."

"Well . . . you could sleep in here. We could keep our clothes on and just cover up with the duvet."

"Okay," he said so rapidly that she responded quickly with, "But no kissing." She knew that would lead to actions she was just not ready for.

"Okay," he repeated more slowly.

They lay down, both on their backs. He reached out and shut off the lamp.

They lay there and listened to the storm. After a few minutes, he said in a child-like voice, "I'm scared."

She laughed.

In his normal voice, he said, "Could we spoon? No kissing, I promise. Or anything else inappropriate."

Annie's heart did a highland fling against her ribs. "Okay."

His tall frame allowed him to rest one arm above her head while she leaned back against his chest. He draped his other arm around her waist. They molded together as if they were custom-fit for one another.

"Is my arm too heavy?" He whispered the words into her ear.

"No, it's fine." To her surprise, she realized she didn't

want more. Or need more. She felt safe. It seemed like a lifetime ago that someone had held her like this.

Then she heard something other than the wind: a snore. It was soft, non-invasive. He had fallen asleep.

She wanted to just lie there awake so she could prolong this moment, enjoy every second. But way too soon, she drifted off.

CHAPTER TWELVE

Annie peered between the wipers. Sometime in the night, consistent with the region's flip-flop weather, the temperatures had risen. The snow had turned to rain, changing the once brilliant white landscape to a dirty grey.

At Jonathan's she had awoken to solitude not solaced by the smell of coffee and toast. Wary of her bed-styled hair and morning face, she timidly came down the stairs.

He seemed tense and his smile and offer of breakfast could not dispel that. She declined food and offered to change into the clothes she had worn to the rink. His response led her into a somewhat brighter world.

He stepped close and put his arms about her waist. "No, you wear them home," he said in that soft voice of his. "That way you'll have to bring them back." His kiss was brief, but long enough to tell her he would be very pleased if she did just that.

So she left, with this hint of a promise that she would see him again in the New Year. And like their spooning the night before, it was all she needed. For now, at least.

She turned onto her street and noticed a police car parked in her driveway behind Dette's old Honda.

Good Lord, what now? As the already narrow street had been compromised further by the snowbanks the plows had made, Annie parked as close to the grey stuff as she could, hoping the curb was lurking in there somewhere.

She got out of her car and wondered what curve ball fate had thrown her this time, just when the future had begun to look a little less clouded. The cop, a female, stood chatting in the doorway. Dette pointed towards her and the cop turned to look at Annie.

"What's up?" Annie said to Dette as she climbed the steps to get out of the annoying rain.

"This is Constable Fennell." Dette made a sweeping motion towards Annie. "May I present the infamous Annie Terrell?"

Infamous? Annie offered her hand, which the policewoman declined.

"May I see some identification please?"

Oh shit, what now? Annie thought. After a quick search of her coat pockets she started to panic then remembered she had left her driver's license in her vehicle in lieu of taking anything valuable into the rink in Baddeck. "It's in my car," she said and hopped off the step.

At least I hope it is, she thought as she jogged through the rain. When she turned to open her car door, she noticed the cop had started to follow her, a startled look on her firm features. Annie could hear Dette say something then laugh. Whatever it was, the cop returned to the porch walking backwards, as if she wanted to keep an eye on Annie.

Did she think I was going to flee or something? Annie wondered. She ran back to the porch and handed her license to the cop. After a long moment of scrutiny, the constable returned it to Annie.

"Are you aware that you are required to obtain a Nova Scotia license within three months of moving here?"

"Yes," Annie lied. Oh shit. Have they nothing better to do than chase down Ontarians who don't belong here?

Just then a voice sputtered from a mic pinned to the shoulder of the cop's coat. She tipped her hat and with a "Have a nice day, Mrs. Terrell," she headed to her car, tilting her head sideways as she muttered into her mic.

Before Annie could ask what the hell was going on, Dette said in a lowered tone. "Will you look at that?"

Annie followed Dette's narrowed gaze to the cop who was now getting into her car.

"What?"

"An ass so hard I could bounce hockey pucks off of it, I'm sure I could."

Annie sighed. "Well, she probably wouldn't appreciate that."

Dette grinned. "Don't be so sure."

"Don't be so crude. And get out of the way so I can close the door. Furnace oil doesn't grow on trees, you know. And tell me what the hell that was all about."

"First, tell me about your night."

"Nothing happened. Shit. I left my hockey bag in the car."

Dette's eyebrows shot up in disbelief. "Didn't you spend the night at Jonathan's?"

"I did and I will fill you in on a few details if you tell me why that cop was looking for me."

"Okay, okay. I guess someone in Toronto misses ya. Some lady got worried when they hadn't heard a peep from you, got talking to some other friend, and they wanted to make sure you got here okay. They contacted the Sydney police and I guess Ms. Fennell got the short straw and was told to follow up on it. You know, you really should get a phone, Antsy."

"You're probably right."

"Well, you obviously forget how to use one, else you would have used Jonathan's to call and tell me you wouldn't be home until today. And, speaking of which, 'fess up. Ooh, by that smile tuggin' at yer face and yer bright eyes, I take it was a good night?"

"It was very nice. Not much to tell. Other than him cooking me supper, nothing happened."

Her eyebrows danced. "Nothing?"

"Maybe a kiss or two." Annie decided to keep the warm memory of the spooning to herself.

"Ach, what a gentleman. Probably just taking it slow. Besides, we're already into the mistletoe season."

"I won't see him until the New Year. He and his family are joining his son in Vancouver for the holidays."

"Ah well, anticipation makes the heart grow hornier, so they say."

"So you say."

"How about, as soon as ya gets yer gear inside, we get that master bedroom floor ready for the sanding machine? I've only got a couple of hours before I head into work."

Annie paused. Something was missing. Then, she felt it. That heavy feeling, though still there, lingered in the shadows, as if waiting to be beckoned. But she knew that to keep it at bay through this darkest of all seasons, she would be able to turn to thoughts of Jonathan, his pending return, and of what could potentially happen then.

* * * *

"Dette, the plan was for me to come over for Christmas dinner. Not Christmas Eve."

But her friend ignored Annie and proceeded to go through Annie's underwear drawer. She held up a panty and peered through a hole. "Antsy, I really oughta take ya shoppin' and I hates shopping. Before Jonathan comes back at least."

Annie grabbed the panty from Dette. "I don't do Christmas, remember? You should be home with Gran."

Dette swung about, her black eyes glittering with either real anger or just impatience, maybe a bit of both. "Jesus Christ, Annie! Who d'ya think sent me out in this shitty weather? Rain one minute, snow the next. Now the temperature's dropping and black ice will soon be turnin' the roads into rinks."

"Thanks, Dette." Annie softened her tone with gratitude, which was easy, as she was grateful. "But I really want to stay here, because of the Christmas thing, but also because I don't want to leave Temp alone."

"Gran says to bring Temp. And I ain't leaving here without either of you. Aha!" A root of Annie's closet resulted in the discovery of a small tote bag, which Dette tossed onto the bed. "Grab a change of clothes and get yer ass downstairs before I haul it down."

When Dette turned back at the doorway, her features had softened. "Look, all ya gotta do is eat something, then drink a couple of Gran's triple-rum-laced eggnogs, then go put yer foggy head on a pillow. Believe me, that's all it'll take to clear yer brain of coherent thoughts, even of the hunky doc."

Guilt washed over Annie and built on a dark tide that threatened to pull her into the mire of depression that had plagued her the past two Christmases.

It'll be all right.

This return of the whisper was enough to push Annie

into action. She shoved her best jeans and nicest sweater into the tote.

She was just about to head towards the stairs when Dette hollered, "Antsy! Get yer arse down here! Temp's in her carrier and she's not liking it."

"I'm coming!"

When she reached the bottom of the stairs, Annie asked, "Want to take my car?" Her all-wheel drive vehicle might prove safer on the slippery roads.

"Only if you let me drive," Dette said as she cradled the carrier.

"Sure." Annie took the cat tote and held it up at face level. "It's okay, Temp. We're not going to the vet."

With an unhappy Temp mewling in the back seat, Dette drove the Subaru towards the community the locals referred to as The Pier.

The rain had been replaced by soft large snowflakes that soon created a scene fit for a Christmas movie. The houses in the area were traditionally small but they were more decorated for Christmas than the rest of the city, most of them in a haphazard way, as if each year the owners added new lights and decorations to the previous years'. Dette's entire street cast brilliant, multi-colored hues into the sky.

The moment Annie stepped inside the door, Gran wrapped her arms around Annie with such a welcoming warmth that Annie had to fight a sudden urge to cry.

Gran seemed to sense this as she abruptly pulled away and stooped to coo at the newly freed Temp as if the cat was a precious infant. "I've some treats for you, I do. Here, come with me, they're in the kitchen."

Dette's eyes followed Gran a moment, then turned on Annie. "Thanks for comin'. I know this time of year is not easy for ya, but, man, I haven't seen Gran so excited about Christmas in years. The past few days, she almost seemed like her old self, cooking and ordering me about."

Gran reappeared in the kitchen doorway "Show Flora Ann to her room, then get yourselves into the kitchen. I'll start setting food on the table."

Dette picked up Annie's overnight bag and led Annie down the narrow hallway to a room at the back of the house. She threw the bag onto the bed. "Now, let's get into some serious Christmas cheer."

Annie shook her head. "But that's your bed or are you planning on sharing it with me?"

Dette grinned. "Yer not that lucky, my friend. I'm crashing on the couch."

"No way!" Annie said, but Dette ignored her and headed out of the room, speaking over her shoulder. "Gran wouldn't put up with that. Besides, this way I might get to see Santa come, sleepin' in front of the tree like that."

This made Annie put on the brakes. "Dette, we said no presents, remember? You promised."

"Down, girl. Don't worry, no presents. Gran wanted to, but I told her your feelings about Christmas and that no way would you step a foot inside this house if you thought we might have bought or made you something. So come on out to the kitchen and at least let Gran feed you."

Like the decorations that adorned every available surface, the table was equally laden with food, each plate and dish wedged tightly against its neighbour. Three kinds of perogis, a steaming bowl of mushroom sauce, a whole stuffed salmon, baked beans, fish cakes, and biscuits. On the cupboard counter stood two pies, a fruitcake, and a three-tiered platter stacked with all kinds of squares.

"Gran, this is a feast," Annie said.

Gran pointed to the cupboard. "Grab yourself a plate and load it up, then find yourself a seat on the sofa. Dette will bring ye in a drink."

"What be your poison, Antsy? Hot rum toddy or . . . ," Dette pulled a bottle of white wine out of the fridge and held it aloft.

"Oh shit, I should have brought wine. Your fault, rushing me like you did," she said to Dette who was in the process of pulling the cork.

"We've got loads. Gran, what do you want to drink?"

Gran frowned a moment, then said, "You know, I think I'd like a wee bit of whatever Flora Ann is having." She winked at Annie. "Broaden me horizons, so to speak."

With a full plate on her lap and a glass of wine at her elbow, Annie looked at the impossibly full tree that took up nearly half of the small room. Nostalgia hung from every limb and Celtic Christmas music poured out of a CD player parked beneath the tree.

Temp was already curled up asleep at the other end of the couch, as if she'd claimed the space as hers.

Annie and Gil, being the atheists they were, had never embraced Christmas traditions. Sure, they had gone to staff and friends' Christmas parties, but as far as decorating and gift giving went, they abstained, choosing instead to make a sizeable donation to a different charity each year. They had always spent Christmas doing whatever they felt like doing, always together, giving each other the gift of time. It was that, she realized, that had made Christmas special.

And now here she was, celebrating as she had as a child. Her best memories of Christmases were the ones when Kaitlyn was still alive. Although her sister was several years older, Annie remembered how excited Kaitlyn would get. She would tell Annie tales of Santa and would wake Annie before dawn so they could sneak down to see if there were presents under the tree.

After Kaitlyn died, all happiness seemed to follow her to the grave. Though Annie was ten at the time and must have learned the truth behind Santa Clause before then, that first Christmas without her sister held no magic and everything seemed so fake.

After that Annie questioned everything her parents said and the more she questioned, the more they insisted she should just do what they said without argument. She could not wait to cast their smothering cloak and escape to university. She'd chosen a university in Toronto primarily because that was where Kaitlyn had died.

"Drink up, Antsy, and I'll give ya a refill." Dette stood in front of her, reaching for her glass.

"You don't have to wait on me," she said.

"Yes, I do," Dette said, tossing her head in the direction of Gran, who was chomping into a perogi and trying to smile at Annie at the same time.

The few sips of wine had already softened Annie's anti-Christmas resolve, and she soaked in the colors, the music, the food, and the grin on Dette's face. She lifted her glass to toast these dear friends.

"Thank-you, to both of you."

"Merry Christmas, Antsy," Dette said.

And it was.

CHAPTER THIRTEEN

Annie tried to open her eyes but it felt as if someone was sitting on them. She somehow managed to pry open her left eye. Then she tried her right one. After deciding that the left eye could open a little more, she used that one to look at her watch, an action that created a throb behind her left temple. She was not sure, as her eye had trouble focusing, but she thought it told her it was just past eleven.

She bolted upright and found herself in a strange bed. Dette's bed. She looked at her watch with both eyes now. Yep, it was seven minutes after eleven a.m. Bright sun blasted through the sheer curtains as if yelling at her that she had spent most of Christmas morning sleeping.

She flung her legs over the bed and stood up. More protests from her head brought back memories of the night before. She had finished off the bottle of wine that she and Gran had started, except Gran had only imbibed half a glass, if Annie's foggy memory could be trusted.

Then, after sampling both the blueberry and mincemeat pies, they returned to the living room. With the curtains opened to Mother Nature's stage upon which a wintry battle played out, they began rounds of toddies. Hot, buttery, rum toddies that tasted like liquid toffee. This was followed by stories from Gran and a few from Dette, midst innumerable giggles and guffaws. Annie barely remembered climbing into bed, let alone falling asleep.

Temp was nowhere to be seen, but Annie suspected her pet was curled up sleeping somewhere after being so spoiled she would not want to leave here.

Annie heard muted chatter from the living room and stole to the bathroom for first aid of the cosmetic variety. Hung over as she was, something positive still rode within her. Satisfaction? No. Stability? No. Well-being.

That was it. A sense of feeling better. Not physically, her queasy stomach was a testament to that, but mentally more sound, thanks to the terrific therapy of the night before.

She did a finger brush of her hair and straightened her wrinkled shirt that she had slept in, and, feeling like a naughty teen-ager that got away with something, she entered the living room to find three strangers staring at her.

Oh shit, she thought, and wanted to bolt, but it was too late.

"Antsy!" Dette said from behind her. "About time you got up! Worried you were going to sleep through Christmas, I was." Dette set down a tray laden with cups and saucers and what Annie guessed to be a teapot hiding beneath a flowered cozy. "This here's my cousin Eleanor and her husband, Frank, and their daughter, Flossie." The couple appeared to be in their seventies. Their daughter, a middle-aged woman, stood up to shake hands with Annie.

The parents were dressed in what looked like their Sunday best, but Flossie wore a thick hand-knit sweater with dancing reindeer on the front and a pair of jeans, which helped Annie feel a little less conspicuous.

"Merry Christmas," Flossie said.

Annie murmured an echo, then backed out of the room as she excused herself to go help Gran. She found her in the kitchen basting an already brown turkey that looked huge compared to Gran's tiny frame.

She smiled at Annie. "Oh, good morning, Flora Ann. Did you sleep well?"

"Too well. I should have been up helping you with dinner. And if I'd known you were having company . . ."

"You'd what?" Dette said as she entered the kitchen. "Tch, Annie, don't fret. Me cousins are in town just till tomorrow and they won't be staying long as they've lots more cousins to see." She poured more milk into the little pitcher that matched the flowered sugar bowl, then took both into the living room.

"Set this bird back into the oven for me, will you?" Gran asked Annie.

The heavy aroma of turkey made Annie hungry in spite of her iffy stomach.

Gran whisked off her apron. "Now, I'm going in to chat with me company for a bit. You have some tea and toast so your stomach will forget all about those toddies by the time we sit down to Christmas dinner."

Annie was still following these instructions when their company walked past on their way to the front door. They tossed season greetings into the kitchen.

After they were gone, Gran said to Dette, "Start your car, will you, dearie, so's it'll be warm?"

"Uh, Gran, my car is at Annie's."

"Use mine," Annie said.

"Why thank you, Flora Ann."

"A quick midday service, is all," Dette said. "It won't last more'n half an hour."

Gran turned her rheumy eyes to Annie. "You'll come with us, Flora Ann, won't you?"

"Uh, I'm not really dressed for church."

Dette waved a dismissal. "I'm wearing me jeans. No one dresses up for church these days."

Annie pointedly looked at the silken dress Gran had on.

"Cept the older generations," Dette added. She tossed Annie her coat. "C'mon, God doesn't bite."

Annie refrained from commenting that to two-thirds of the population, she and Dette would be considered an older generation. Though church was the last place she wanted to be, the smile that Gran gave Annie when she pulled on her coat was so warm and full of love that Annie realized that any discomfort or hypocrisy she would feel would be a small price to pay for any amount of joy she could give this kind woman.

But the moment Annie stepped inside the tiny, old church, doubt began to weave its gnarly web. She was grateful the only seats left were at the very back as too many people had already turned in their seats and glanced their way. Their smiles and nods did little to erase Annie's feeling that she had "heathen" branded into her forehead.

She studied the program in her hand and wished they were at the benediction point.

When the congregation rose and began to sing "The First Noel," Annie only mouthed the words and could not help but glance around.

The place was packed, the air heavy. Most here would find the atmosphere warm and spiritual and in the ensuing sermon hints of possibility and hope. But Annie did not believe the minister's words.

Gil was gone. Gone forever, and the fact that she could not believe in an afterlife made her feel like the ultimate outsider. Among these people, she was as alone as if she were adrift on flotsam in an endless ocean.

To her alarm, she felt tears coursing down her cheeks.

She hastily wiped her face then heard Dette clear her throat. When Dette cleared her throat a second time, Annie braved a glance at her friend. Dette motioned with her head towards the door and Annie nodded.

"Excuse me?" she whispered to Gran, fearful she would offend her.

But Gran only smiled, squeezed her hand and nodded.

Dette followed Annie out into the vestibule, her dark brows knit in worry. "You okay, Antsy?"

Her friend's sympathy forced open another floodgate. Annie forced a smile through her tears. "I don't know what's wrong with me."

"This time of year is always either extremely joyful or extremely painful. Jesus, haven't you watched any Christmas movies?"

Annie could not help but smile. "Gran would tan your hide for swearing in a church."

Dette reached inside her coat and pulled out three envelopes tied together with ribbon. "I was going to give you these when I took you back home tonight, but maybe you'll want to read them now whilst you wait for the service to finish."

"What are they?"

"Letters sent to the police station. Gwen gave me them to give to you."

"Gwen?"

"Constable Fennell." Dette pointed to the cards. "They're from your friends in Toronto. The ones who can't call you because you don't own a frigging phone. The same ones you haven't given your new address to." She squeezed Annie's arm. "Sermon shouldn't last more'n twenty minutes. See ya then."

Annie lowered herself onto a bench and began to

open the envelopes. All Christmas cards from the feel of them. The first one contained a letter from a former teammate, saying she still missed Annie on her wing. Another card was from a fellow writer who had belonged to her writing circle. The third one was from a former friend and colleague of Gil who had urged Annie to keep in touch.

Annie gathered the three envelopes together in her lap. She had hardly seen or talked to these people since Gil had died and still, they sought to find her, to see how she was doing.

Tears begin to fall again, and although she was the only person in the foyer, she realized she was no more alone than those singing their hearts out inside.

CHAPTER FOURTEEN

Annie slowly sipped her wine. If she did otherwise, she knew she would be too intoxicated to appreciate the arrival of the New Year. She had only been at Colleen's for a little over two hours and the other members of the Dames hockey team, seasoned drinkers that they were, appeared to be hardly feeling the effects of the copious amounts of alcohol they had imbibed.

Dette met her eye from across the room and they raised their glasses in a silent salute. Annie was glad her friend talked her into coming. The hockey women were a boisterous, comedic bunch with at least two of them funny enough to do stand-up for a living.

Annie hadn't minded the odd teasing barb about her and Jonathan, though she had ignored specific questions, partly because she did not want to propagate idle gossip at Jonathan's expense and partly because she could not be certain if Jonathan would pick up where he left off once he returned.

In the meantime, she let herself enjoy the anticipation of seeing him again. Between that and Dette and Gran including her in their festivities, she had not fallen into the dark mire of past Christmases.

She glanced again at Dette, who seemed more animated than usual tonight and Annie suspected the reason for this was the woman sitting beside her: Constable Gwen Fennell. Dette had recruited the young woman to the hockey team and although Gwen had not played hockey since high school, the gal's obvious fitness and hard work ethic already rendered her one of the better players.

"Yer lookin' a little smiley, Antsy!" Dette had to holler to be heard above the catcalls and whistles coming from the girls parked in front of the television as they watched a racy romantic comedy that on occasion briefly tiptoed across the border into pornography.

Annie held up her glass. "I am, thanks to this."

"Is it that or are yer thoughts wandering to Jon-a-than?" Dette elongated the name, emphasizing each syllable.

Colleen, being the proper Cape Breton hostess she was, handed out shots, clear ones this time: tequila, or something worse. She leaned over to whisper to Annie. "Is that Dr. Dooley you're talking about?" Colleen was the player who worked as a receptionist at the clinic and had gotten Annie that first appointment.

When Annie nodded, Colleen's features sobered with concern before she ducked back into the kitchen. Her worried look lingered in Annie's mind and eroded her festive mood to the point that she had no choice but to seek out Colleen in the kitchen. She found her standing at the sink, washing used shot glasses.

Without a word, Annie picked up a tea towel and started to dry. After a long moment, Colleen turned to her.

"How involved are you with Dr. Dooley?" she asked

and then turned away with a shake of her head. "Sorry, it's none of my business and I've no right to ask."

Annie wasn't sure how to answer her. Physically, beyond the few kisses, she was hardly involved. Emotionally, however, judging by the way her throat tightened, Annie realized she had already waded too deep into waters she had sworn to avoid after losing Gil.

Colleen turned back to face her and spoke in a low voice. "Look, Annie, I like you. You seem really nice and I don't want to see you get hurt. If you are serious about him, there's something you should know."

Annie swallowed in an attempt to clear her constricting throat. She managed to croak out, "What is it?"

Colleen sighed, dried her hands, and placed them on her hips. "Well, when Dr. Dooley first came here three years ago . . . " She paused a moment before continuing, "Anyway, when he came here, he did not come alone."

She studied Annie closely as if checking to see if she should continue. Annie forced a blank expression onto her features while alarm bells rang so loudly inside her head she feared her skull was visibly pulsing.

"Vivian was her name, I think. Man, I hate this menopausal memory of mine. Anyway, she was a social worker who worked at the Cape Breton Regional Hospital, at least while she was here. Rumour has it that she and Dr. Dooley had been living together out in Edmonton. Well, she lasted only six months here and since then . . . well, since then she's been coming here on occasion to visit him and he's been going to Edmonton to see her."

Annie forced air into resistant lungs. It all made sense. The nicely decorated home. The makeup in the drawer. Dammit, why had he kissed her? Monogamous puppy that she was, Annie had always considered anything beyond a casual hug to be cheating. A thought pierced her already troubled mind.

"Is he in Edmonton now?" Over New Years? Annie had assumed that he would be staying with his son in Vancouver until he returned.

Colleen's eyes rounded with sympathy. "Probably. Oh man, I hope you don't mind me telling you this."

Annie surprised herself by being able to smile. "I'm glad you did." And she was. Better to know now than before anything physical did happen.

"So you're okay?" Colleen looked so worried that Annie wondered if she knew Annie had spent a night with Jonathan.

"Nothing has happened between us," Annie said, wanting to clarify the rumors that she suspected would spread after tonight. "We've kissed a few times, that's all. Thanks for giving me the heads up."

Colleen did not look convinced.

Annie forced a laugh and allowed herself to use a cliché. "Nipped in the bud! Now how about making more of those shooters?"

When the clock struck twelve, everyone hugged, except for Dette and Gwen, who did a quick peck. Annie had partaken in the shooters and though the alcohol cruising through her veins made the room spin when she closed her eyes, it could not block out the image she had of what Jonathan was probably doing at that very moment: kissing someone named Vivian. Something wet ran down her cheeks and she headed for the bathroom. There, she cried so hard she became nauseated.

Someone pounded on the door. "Antsy, you okay?"

"Yep," she lied. She swallowed against the nausea. "Just too much to drink," which certainly had not helped things.

"Colleen just filled the rest of us in. C'mon, open the

door."

"No, I'm fine. Too many of those goddamn shooters." Annie looked in the mirror to see a portrait of a grieving, aging widow. She plastered on a smile and opened the door while she could still hold it on her face. "See? I'm fine."

"Then why are you crying?"

Annie returned to the mirror and Dette was right, the tears were still flowing. She closed the toilet lid and sank down onto it, her head in her hands. She heard the door shut and felt Dette squat beside her. The palpable sympathy in the air triggered another round of sobbing.

Annie wiped at her face and straightened up. "This is ridiculous," she said, then blew her nose. "Nothing happened. We had, what, one date? One cuddle? A few kisses?"

"Antsy, you don't know the whole story. Maybe they've agreed to start seeing other people."

"And maybe he's kissing her right now. Shit!"

"So what if he is? That doesn't necessarily mean things have to stop between you two."

Annie turned her head so she could look Dette in the eye. "Oh, but it does, my friend. I will not share any man. I will not share even the promise of him."

"Oh, Antsy, you have fallen hard, haven't you?"

Sorrow flooded Annie, stirring her stomach further. In quick, jerky movements, Annie swung her butt off the seat, lifted the lid, and let her stomach have its way. She accepted the washcloth Dette dampened for her and wiped her mouth.

"Wine and shooters don't mix too well," she said.

"That they don't," Dette agreed.

But an inner voice warned Annie that her stomach had reacted the exact same way when Gil was first diagnosed and again on the day he passed away. Another loss? Is this her way of coping: purging grief in a physical way?

Accept it and move on, she told herself. Even her whisper would be welcome. It seemed the only time she didn't hear those words of hope was when she needed them most.

She washed her face at the sink and in the mirror saw Dette still hovering behind her. Both gratitude and a quiet tummy instilled a calm in her. It was all good news, she told herself. She was free to get that damn house ready to sell and return to her other life in Toronto.

Fully independent.

Fully in control.

CHAPTER FIFTEEN

The first co-ed shinny after the New Year fell on the third of January, a little less than sixty hours after Annie found out about Jonathan's seemingly significant other. He had popped into her thoughts frequently, but other than rehearsing a speech to spew when she saw him, she had been able to staunchly suppress thoughts of him by keeping busy with the house repairs.

When he did not show up for shinny, her relief conflicted with impatience to get the confrontation over with.

The moment Annie stepped outside the arena, her eyes were drawn to her car. As before, and as if he belonged there, Jonathan leaned against her Subaru, squinting against a brilliant sun made more incandescent by the landscape of snow. His open jacket, an indication of the unusually warm temperature, revealed the shirt and tie he probably donned for work at the clinic.

His easy smile nearly melted her resolve to remain distant, so she reminded herself of the burn she had felt on New Year's Eve. She ignored his greeting and avoided eye contact.

She pushed the button to unlock the doors, then had to wait for him to step out of the way so she could open the rear hatch. She threw her hockey bag in with exaggerated enthusiasm.

"What's wrong?" he asked.

She ignored him and slammed the door shut, again with more force than was necessary, and headed towards the driver's door.

He grabbed her elbow, and she wondered again how the warmth of his gentle touch could penetrate through the padded fabric of her winter jacket.

He gently spun her around to face him. Without another word, he lowered his head to kiss her, as if this would fix everything, and for an insane instant, Annie felt like it would. Before his lips met hers she managed to gather enough resolve to pull away.

His brown eyes held a hint of surprise. "Are you okay?"

"Does Vivian know you're kissing me?" she asked.

He leaned back, his eyebrows arching briefly before settling into a frown. "No," he said softly. The guilt in his tone matched his darkening gaze.

"All righty then," Annie said with feigned gaiety and dove into the driver's seat. She locked the door, the click barely audible above her thudding heart.

An irrational part of her hoped he would make a move to stop her from leaving the parking lot. But he just stood there while she maneuvered her vehicle around him, his entire posture exuding an undeniable sadness.

Well, I am sad too, she thought. She headed towards home with an all-too-familiar weight seeping into her heart.

She felt numb by the time she pulled into her driveway. She had been through worse, she reminded herself yet again. The absolute worst. She could surely handle rejection from a man she hardly knew.

She hauled her hockey bag to the back porch to air out her gear before her ebbing energy reached low tide.

When she returned back inside, Temp curled around her leg and purred loudly as if to say, 'See, I still love you.' Annie picked up the feline and hugged her.

Then the whisper returned.

It will be all right.

Yes it will, Annie told herself. She would make it all right.

A loud thunk from the living room startled Temp out of her arms. A breeze passed through the kitchen, the chill air sharp. She entered the living room to find the front door fully open to the unwelcome winter.

She closed the door with considerable resistance from a new-borne wind that pushed fine snowflakes ahead of it. At the rink, the weather had been so nice. She pushed aside an image of Jonathan leaning against her car and engaged the deadbolt with deliberation.

Then she spotted a white envelope on the floor, no doubt disturbed from the mantel by the wind. Aunt Jessie's note from beyond the grave. Annie was supposed to have opened it New Year's Day, but she had totally forgotten about it, most likely because of her obsession with Jonathan. Well, enough of that, she thought.

She took the envelope to the kitchen and used a butter knife to open it. As Annie slid out a folded piece of paper, another single rectangular piece floated out. The fact that it looked like a cheque made Annie grab it before it hit the floor, telling herself all the while that it could not possibly be one.

But it was indeed a cheque for ten thousand dollars, made out to Annie Terrell, from the estate of Jessie MacDonald. Annie then unfolded the note, eager for the answers to the myriad of questions tripping over each other in her head.

The script was beautiful and flawless and made Annie recall that Jessie had been a schoolteacher, the classic old maid of schoolmarms of yesteryear.

Dear Flora Ann.

By now three months have passed since you regained possession of the house that was rightfully yours all these years. I do appreciate you letting me stay here after the demise of your parents, though the house would have stood empty had you not done so.

If young Mr. MacPhee has followed my instructions to the letter, you have owned this house three months and have not yet attempted to sell it.

Whether you are here or in Toronto is of no consequence. Although you may not yet realize it, this house is a home but it requires renovations. It is my wish that the funds enclosed be spent on such. I do know that requesting this may result in you doing otherwise even though by now you are a middle-aged woman and childish rebellion should be beyond you.

Annie paused to swallow the sour taste of the chiding, which, in spite of her so-called maturity, did make her want to rebel. Time softened only some memories, she decided, and read on.

I harbour the hope that you will spend both the money and some time repairing your childhood home in person. Perhaps during the process, you will recall some of the happier moments spent here, and will remember that this has been a place where you were cherished.

I also realize that with your husband's passing, this sum of money may seem inconsequential to you and may do nothing to assuage your pain or to encourage you to give your home the attention it needs.

And thus, with an old spinster's softening heart, I bid you good-bye.

Just remember this: you were loved.

By us all.

Loved? Cherished? Happy moments? If Annie really dug a deep ditch into her past, she could recall a few birthdays, even fewer Christmases, and the rare picnic where she might have been happy.

But all of those memories had one common denominator: the presence of her sister Kaitlyn. And in all of them she could recall a thread of unease between her sister and their parents. Later, after Kaitlyn's death, this tension seemed to be redirected towards Annie. And it thickened even more after Aunt Jessie came to live with them.

Annie still marveled at the strong, loving relationship she and Kaitlyn had forged, in spite of the twelve (or was it fourteen?) years difference in age between them. Then again, she had seen it with friends: how children who are nearly baby-sitting age appear to enjoy much younger siblings. And perhaps she had provided Kaitlyn a reprieve from the controlling net their parents cast over them.

She sighed and studied the cheque. Ten thousand dollars. It must have been hard for Jessie to squirrel away such a sum. She resolved to do as Jessie wanted. She would use it to fix up the house, but that did not mean she would ever consider staying here.

Annie reached down to pet Temp who had begun to curl around Annie's leg. What should she do first? Pay down her loan or spend it directly on the house? Spend it on the house, she decided. New siding on the outside would certainly raise the value of the place.

An urge to call Dette put one thing at the top of her list. She would get a cell phone. She would go to the bank, deposit this baby, and then visit the phone company. Then she would stop by Home Depot and see if Dette could get off work early so Annie could take her to dinner.

This idea blossomed into a plan. She'd take a couple hundred dollars from this and take Dette to the casino for a night of supper, drinks, and a bit of gambling fun. She owed Dette this, she rationalized, even if Jessie wouldn't approve.

Annie pulled on her coat with a lightness she had not felt since finding out about Vivian.

CHAPTER SIXTEEN

"Annie?"

Annie stopped sipping her wine and looked up and to her left. The handsome face of Aunt Jessie's lawyer smiled down at her.

He probably suspected she was feeding all of Aunt Jessie's hard-saved cash into the machine in front of her, but, at the moment, emboldened by her third glass of wine, Annie didn't care. In truth, she was throwing a bit of Jessie's money away, but not that much, as Dette and she had won enough here and there to keep playing. So, guilt-free, she returned his smile.

"You didn't call, so I assumed you didn't have any questions for me after opening the note."

Annie shook her head a little too vigorously, so she focused on appearing sober and semi-intelligent. "Thank-you, though. How was the skiing?"

"Wonderful. We stayed at Sunshine in Banff. The snow there is one hundred per cent natural. Problem is, I couldn't keep up with my kids."

Annie's brain had trouble keeping up with his words.

To show she was listening, she asked, "How old are they?"

"Twelve and fifteen." He pointed to the empty seat beside her. "May I sit down?"

Knowing Dette would return at any moment to rescue her, Annie gracefully (or at least in her current inebriated state it felt graceful enough) waved her arm in acceptance. She randomly punched the times-two button then turned back to Denny. "Teenagers. How fun."

He shrugged. "They live with their mother in Edmonton. I see them only at Christmas and for summer holidays so if they act up I can blame her."

Edmonton. Where Jonathan went. To be with Vivian. Annie kept her smile on as she pushed the times-three button, a splurge that raised her bet to seventy-five cents.

"You don't remember me, do you?" Denny asked.

She pulled her attention away from the screen. "Excuse me?"

"From high school. I was a year behind you." He raised his eyebrows. "I was shorter then. But after I turned eighteen I grew five inches."

Annie allowed herself a grimace. "Sorry. Don't take offence, but I wasn't a happy camper in high school and concentrated on escaping to university."

He smiled. "No offence taken. I was not big enough to partake in most of the sports, but I did watch a lot. I remember you from the field hockey team. And didn't you score the winning goal when the girls played ice hockey against Glace Bay?"

Annie frowned then laughed when she recalled the game. "Oh yeah. We had to wear the boy's large, stinky gear. The pants fell below my knees. I could hardly skate."

He shook his head. "That's not how I remember it. That year the boys' varsity team sucked and Glace Bay constantly kicked our ass. The stands were filled that night and you made a lot of Academy boys happy by scoring that goal late in the third."

"Wow, your memory is better than mine."

"I also sat behind you in math."

Annie squinted at him, wondering how she could have not noticed this good-looking guy in school. "I thought you said you were a year behind me."

"I excelled in a few courses and was able to jump ahead in math and chemistry." A flush tinted his cheeks.

Modest, as well as good-looking, Annie thought.

Dette materialized behind them with an abruptness that made Annie jump. "Wee Denny!" She clapped him heartily on the back. "How the hell are ya?"

He stood up. "Fine . . . er, I didn't mean to interrupt." He looked from Annie to Dette, then said, "Um . . . are you two . . . you know?"

Dette's roar made several of the surrounding patrons look to see how much they might have won. "Oh, no, Den. I'm gay, but Annie here is as straight as a ruler."

This last statement made the other gamblers swiftly turn back to their own machines.

Denny kept his gaze on Annie and she realized his eyes were a dark brown. Not a soft brown like . . . she sighed.

"Sorry, I didn't mean to offend you," Denny said, obviously misunderstanding her sigh.

"No, no offence taken."

"Can I call you sometime?" he asked Annie.

"Sure you can," Dette said. "She's absolutely available." She elbowed Annie in the ribs. "Give him your cell phone number, Antsy."

"Uh, I just got my phone." She worried she was getting senile, as the number remained blurred inside the haze of alcohol. "It's uh . . ."

"227-4319!" Dette said way too loudly. "But you can't text her. She got the free phone with the cheap plan."

Denny pulled out his phone and with fast thumbs punched Annie's number in. He smiled at Annie as he slipped his phone inside his jacket. "Talk to you later then."

After he left, Annie clouted Dette on the shoulder. "What the hell?"

"What? Good thing I'm not too drunk to remember your new number."

"Absolutely available? That sounded like absolutely desperate."

"You do need a man, Antsy. It's written all over yer face, for Chrissakes."

Okay, Annie conceded to herself. Maybe she did need a little action in the romance department. At least it felt like that with alcohol swimming upstream in her veins.

But even in this wine-induced state, she remained certain that if the man she wanted was not available, she would prefer none at all. Not even Denny, as cute as he was.

* * * *

Annie shoved her gear into her bag. She wanted to leave the arena before any of the others, particularly before Jonathan. He hadn't said two words to her during the shinny, even when he made a terrific pass that she deflected into the net.

She peeled off her sweaty top and pulled on her sweatshirt. She would wear wet underwear home if it meant she could avoid running into Jonathan in the parking lot.

A gentle ring came from inside Annie's coat pocket. Her cell phone. She pulled it out of her jacket. "Hello?"

There was no one there.

"Reception here in the rink may not be good, Antsy," Dette said.

Annie glanced at the screen and sure enough it read "Lost Signal." She slid the phone back into her pocket.

Must have been Denny, she thought, as he was the only person other than Dette who had been given her number. She knew he was planning to ask her out and this filled her with more dread than anticipation.

A person always wants what they can't have, she thought, and zipped up her bag. Her post-hockey high was already dissipating.

She waved to Dette and scurried outside only to see Jonathan waiting at the door to the rink. Though he held the door open for her, she pushed past without acknowledging his presence and walked as fast as she could to her vehicle.

His long legs easily kept up. He set down his bag and stick as she once again took out her frustration on both the bag and the rear door of her car.

"You didn't let me explain," he said in that soft voice of his.

She was about to crawl inside her car, but gave in to temptation and whirled about to face him.

"You can't be chasing two rabbits at once," she said, borrowing from a phrase Dette had used.

He sighed. "It's complicated."

"So make it uncomplicated. Go chase the Edmonton rabbit." His close proximity stirred a want in her to kiss him, so she turned away to open her door.

The gentle melody of her cell phone gave her a welcome distraction. She pulled out her phone. "Hello?"

The word came out in a tense gasp.

"Oh, am I interrupting something?" Denny asked.

She turned so she could no longer see Jonathan in the reflection of the driver's side window. "No, you're not interrupting anything. I just finished playing hockey."

Though she still had her back to Jonathan she could feel him retreating.

"I was wondering if you would have dinner with me tonight?"

In a voice that she hoped was loud enough for Jonathan to hear, she said, "Sure. I'd love to have dinner with you." What better way to keep from drowning with Jonathan than to jump in the deep end with Denny?

"I'll pick you up at seven, okay?"

"See you tonight." She slid the phone into her pocket and turned to find Jonathan waiting near the back of her car.

He stepped closer, though a large gap still remained between them. "So you don't want to hear details? Why I didn't tell you about Vivian?"

How much she wanted to hear his explanation bothered her enough that she chose to lie. "No, I don't."

He studied her another long moment, his eyes unchanging, unreadable. Then he turned to leave. She knew by the deliberateness of his movements that he would never approach her again. Never wait by her vehicle again.

This she knew as surely as she also knew that it was the last thing she wanted.

CHAPTER SEVENTEEN

"Do you have to do that now?" Annie asked.

Dette paused with what looked like a miniature crowbar in her hand. She was in the process of removing the staples in the wooden floor in the living room. All the carpets in the house and their collection of dust and dirt that had accumulated over the years had been removed and taken to the dump, along with what was left of the worn underlay.

Before the floors could be sanded, all the staples that had attached the underlay to the floor had to be removed, each one protesting its exit with a screech that made Annie cringe.

"You said you wanted this room done first, Antsy, and I've got tonight free. Ooh, yer not wearing that are ya?"

Annie looked down at her silk shirt and dress pants. They were a few years old, but, other than being a bit loose, still fit her. "What's wrong with this outfit?"

"Makes you look too matronly. You're going on a date for Chrissakes. Wear something hot."

"You know, I think you came here not to work, but to keep tabs on my love life."

Dette grinned. "What love life?"

Annie grimaced as much at Dette's words as what she saw in the mirror in the front hallway. The dry winter air had sapped some of the life from her hair and she had to put more product in it to make it appear fuller. This did sort of work but her hair had no sheen, her eyes no sparkle.

It will be all right.

Annie sighed.

Dette's image appeared in the mirror beside Annie. "You don't look that bad."

"You know, I don't think I'm ready to date."

"Says the woman who spent a full night with Dr. Dooley. You sure you've told me everything?"

Annie turned to study her profile in the mirror, which only confirmed her original assessment: she looked all of her fifty-one years. "I'm lucky if I can remember my cell phone number, let alone what I said to you a month ago." But Annie vividly remembered Jonathan tight against her, his arm about her waist, and her not needing or wanting anything else.

"Antsy!"

Startled, Annie answered, "What?"

"Yer eyes just glazed over. You said nothing happened!"

"Nothing beyond first base." But what a first base, she could not help but think.

Dette draped an arm about her friend and raised her dark brows. "Well, maybe you'll get further than first base tonight."

"I have no desire to."

Dette made a face. "Still suffering from Jonathanitis, I see. Well, give smooth Denny a chance. You never know, he may be the cure."

Annie hauled a pair of shoes out of the closet. They

would not be comfortable and thus an appropriate metaphor for the evening ahead. "You know, I think I feel a sore throat coming on." She glanced at her watch. Six-fifty.

"No." Dette pushed her towards the door. "You're not cancelling now."

Annie resisted. "But I could stay here and help you."

Three knocks on the door made them both jump.

"Oh, no, he's early."

"Maybe not." Dette bounded to the door and opened it to a smiling Gwen. Dette ushered her inside and grinned at Annie. "The cavalry has arrived."

"I see," Annie said. Perhaps pulling up staples wasn't at the top of Dette's agenda after all.

Headlights sent light beams gliding across the walls as a car turned the corner and stopped at the end of the driveway.

"Have fun," Dette said as she handed Annie her coat. "Don't come home before midnight."

Annie suppressed her reluctance and put on the best smile she could as she walked out the door.

* * * *

Denny parked his car at the curb in front of Annie's driveway which was now filled with the three vehicles belonging to Annie, Dette, and Gwen. He turned off the engine and the moment Annie had been dreading all evening arrived.

"Thanks for supper," she said. She had enjoyed Denny's company. He was a smart, considerate man, but she'd been grateful there had been no sparks, no complicating attraction.

"You okay?" Denny asked.

"Yes, why?"

"You sighed."

She hoped her laugh didn't sound as fake as her next words did. "Oh, I'm just a bit tired." She gestured toward the house. "Still fixing the place up."

A thought came to her that was safe ground for conversation. "If Aunt Jessie had that money sitting in the bank, why didn't she fix up the place herself? Or at least buy herself some new appliances?"

"Who knows? She didn't waste words with idle chatter. Very professional. Very old school. Though my guess is that she wanted you to decide to live here after you fixed it up."

Annie gestured again towards the house. "Uh, would you like to come in for some coffee?" Hopefully Gwen and Dette were finished whatever they had planned for the evening.

"Uh, better not." He wrinkled his nose. "Cat allergy."

"Oh I'm sorry. I forgot."

Then Denny did what she had been dreading. When he leaned over the seat toward her and cupped her chin with his hand, she forced herself to relax. The kiss lasted longer than Jonathan's first one and she decided it was a nice first kiss.

But no weak knees. No lip tingles. No whoosh as air filled the space when he pulled away. And definitely no yearning for a repeat.

He leaned back but kept his hand on her chin. "You know, I had a serious crush on you in high school."

"What?" She pulled away from his hand in feigned surprise. "Really?"

Annie recalled being on the outside of the popular groups, below the radar on both looks and personality.

Other than sports she hadn't participated in any of the social events. She didn't even go to the senior prom.

"Yeah. I kinda kept my eye on you."

"Why didn't you ask me out?"

"I was a short little geek. It wasn't until university, after I grew a few inches and bulked up with weights that I gained confidence with girls."

Annie found his self-depreciation attractive. "Then I'll bet the girls fell all over you."

He laughed. "Well, it was a lot different than high school." His smile faded from his face and he leaned towards her again.

She put up a hand. "Denny, I'm sorry."

He cleared his throat. "I prefer Dennis now," he said. "I haven't been called Denny since I left home."

This was the first time he had corrected her, and, strangely, this made her bolder. "Dennis, you are one handsome, nice guy. But . . ."

He sighed. "The infamous but."

"Which, I suspect, you never hear. The truth is, I'm really not ready to date."

"Dette says it's been three years since your husband passed."

"Yes, but I don't think I'll ever be ready." These words felt like a lie, as she had felt ready with Jonathan. She quickly added a truth. "Besides, as soon as the house is market-ready, I'm going to head back to Toronto." She placed a hand on Denny's arm and immediately noticed the lack of warmth. "I think it'd be best if I didn't start a relationship. I'm sorry."

"Don't be. This is my first shot at dating since the divorce. I may not be ready either." He grinned. "Though I feel I am."

She punched his arm playfully. "Then go for it. I'll bet there are lots of women out there looking to date a handsome lawyer. Women who don't have a cat."

He grinned. "Well, I moved here to be closer to my aging parents. Once they're gone, I might go back to Edmonton to be closer to my kids. Hopefully I'll be able to stand being that near my ex." He grinned.

It was a nice grin. And he was a nice man. What's wrong with me? Annie thought. But the relief cruising through her made her realize she had made the right decision.

He walked her to the door and did not try to kiss her again. "You have my number," he said. "Call if you have any questions about your aunt or if you just want to chat about the good old days."

"I will, thanks." But she knew she wouldn't.

Annie unlocked the door and entered a quiet house. She fed a mewling Temp some treats and crept up the stairs to her room. The master bedroom door was closed, but Annie thought she could hear a soft snore emanating from within.

Good for Dette, Annie thought. Then, as she crawled beneath the sheets, the whisper returned.

It will be all right.

Whether it was because she had heard it so often, or perhaps because she was starting to believe it, she found herself in agreement, and settled into the peace that could be always be found beneath thick quilts crafted by caring hands.

* * * *

Ding-dong.

Annie didn't move. She didn't open her eyes. She lay there searching in earnest for the fuzziness of sleep. But those two distinct rings had, like before, pierced her blissfully unaware state to the point of full alert. Why the hell couldn't that doorbell ring at a decent hour of the day?

Probably because she had only dreamt she heard the damn thing, she thought. She angrily yanked her arm from beneath the quilts and exposed it to the cold air just long enough to glance at her watch.

She was surprised to see it was almost nine a.m. She crawled out and hurriedly slipped on sweat pants and a sweater.

This morning the house felt particularly chilly and damp. She glanced out the window at a grey February morning. The sky looked as gloomy as she felt.

She had just reached the bottom step in her hurried journey towards the thermostat when her phone tingled from the mantel. Dette, according to the call display.

"You awake?" Dette asked.

"No, I'm still asleep."

"Well, yer awake enough to be sassy," Dette said. "Sorry to disrupt your beauty rest, and lord knows ya needs it but . . ."

Annie heard the worried tone in her friend's voice. "What's wrong?"

A sigh, then, "Maybe nothing. But I called Gran. She never gets to it before the answering machine kicks in. But she usually phones me right back. It could be nothin' but she hasn't called and me gut is worried. I hate to be a pest, but could you run over and check on her? I can't leave work until noon."

"Of course! I'll go right now."

"Oh thanks, Antsy. Give me a call after you see her, will ya?

"Will do." Annie hung up and pulled on her coat.

With hardly any traffic she was able to reach Gran's in fifteen minutes. She became a little anxious when her loud knock (there was no doorbell here either) failed to initiate any sound from inside the house. She frantically tried the doorknob and sighed with relief when it turned easily.

She lunged inside and yelled, "Gran!"

"In my room," came a very calm reply from down the hall.

Gran lay beneath a knitted afghan on top of her bed. "Don't be in a tither, now. I'm all right. I suppose Bernadette got worried when I didn't call her back. I was going to as soon as I got meself out of bed."

Annie kneeled beside the bed and took Gran's hand in hers. Its warmth calmed her somewhat. "Dette was worried."

A ghost of a smile preceded Gran's words. "I was just a bit dizzy is all. I didn't think I should try to get to the phone, else I could fall and break me hip."

Dizzy didn't sound good. "Maybe I should take you to the hospital," Annie said.

"No, t'is nothing serious as all that. I gets these spells once in a while. If I lay meself down a bit, it'll pass. Maybe it's gone now." She struggled to sit up and Annie reached out to help her.

But just as Gran put her legs over the side, she began to sway and with a long "oooh" she plunked back down.

Annie pulled her phone out. "I'm going to call an ambulance."

Gran grabbed Annie's arm with surprising strength. "No, Flora Ann. If ye needs to call someone, call Jonathan."

The last person Annie wanted to talk to was Jonathan. But Gran's "please" made her punch in the numbers to the clinic.

Gran patted Annie's hand as if to say, "there's a good girl" and closed her eyes.

Annie identified herself to Colleen and asked if she could speak to Dr. Jonathan Dooley concerning Gran.

Jonathan came on the line, listened a moment, then sounded professional and business-like when he responded, "I'll drop over at noon. In the meantime, tell her to stay put and keep an eye on her. If she becomes unresponsive or shows distress of any kind, call 911."

Annie hung up and pulled off her jacket, already too warm. She looked down at her sweats. Then she gave herself a mental slap. It didn't matter how she looked to Jonathan. Not anymore.

Her bladder reminded her it hadn't yet been attended to. As Gran did seem okay, Annie told her she'd be right back and scooted to the nearby bathroom.

In spite of her earlier resolution that her looks didn't matter, she risked a glance in the mirror and couldn't help but frown. Bed-head hair and make-up-less face. Yep, she looked every bit her age, if not older.

So? She asked herself as she retraced her steps back to Gran's room. There was no one she needed to impress.

"Would you like a cup of tea?" she asked Gran.

"That I would, Flora Ann. Would ye be so kind?"

"I would," Annie said, and went to make the tea.

When she returned with what she hoped was tea steeped the appropriate length of time, Gran squirmed to a sitting position and proceeded to sip the brew.

After a few minutes, she abruptly said, "I needs to lie back down." She handed the cup to Annie and slid down until her head rested on the pillow and then she pulled the afghan up to her chin.

Alarmed, Annie leaned over her.

"Tch, don't worry, Flora Ann. I'll just be resting me eyes for a bit."

But Annie did worry and after setting the cup down, she pulled a chair up next to the bed and made sure the afghan-covered chest continued to rise and fall. Her watch proved to be not very long, as two brisk knocks were followed by a "Hello?"

Jonathan was early.

"Come on in," Annie called. "We're in Gran's bedroom." She retreated to the other side of the bed.

Jonathan's broad shoulders were clad in a thick overcoat and they barely cleared the doorway.

Annie wanted to ask why he had arrived so early but she didn't want him to even look at her, let alone talk with her.

He removed his coat and put it over the back of the chair Annie had just vacated, frowning all the while at Gran, who lay as if still sleeping. He wore a suit coat and tie and Annie had to force a wave of attraction away. She made her eyes focus on Gran.

Gran's eyes fluttered open and she gave a brief smile. "What a nuisance I am, Jonathan."

"Hardly," he said as he sat down and pulled a stethoscope out of his bag. "So you've been feeling dizzy, have you?"

"Aye."

He listened to Gran's chest a moment and then took her blood pressure. He shook his head and removed the cuff. "It's a bit low, but not too bad."

Gran pointed to a rocking chair on the opposite side of the bed. "Flora Ann, pull that close so's you can sit and hold my hand. That way I may be able to remain calm while this handsome man is in my bedroom."

Jonathan laughed softly while Annie pulled the rocking chair up next to the bed.

Gran took her hand. Her grip was gentle and yet strong at the same time. Immediately, Annie was struck with a feeling that Gran was okay. She quickly looked at Gran, but the elderly woman was looking at Jonathan.

"Any nausea?" Jonathan asked Gran.

Gran shook her head.

"Any chest pain?"

"No." She reached for his hand. "Thanks so much for coming, dear Jonathan." Then she closed her eyes. But she did not let go of his hand.

At that moment, Annie felt a flush of heat from Gran's hand into hers. It washed through Annie. She looked up and discovered Jonathan's eyes on her. In them, she could see sadness and something else. Something that took her breath away. He had feelings for her. He wanted her. She pulled her gaze to the side before her own eyes responded in a way she was not ready yet to admit to. The heat subsided immediately.

"Gran?" The alarm in Jonathan's voice made Annie look back to the bed. Jonathan was no longer holding her hand, but squeezing her arm.

Gran's chest rose fully and then her eyes fluttered open. Her smile was weak. "I'm fine." She took another deep breath and then answered in a stronger voice. "Really, tis' true. I'm fine now."

Jonathan frowned at her. "Are you sure?"

"Yes, in fact, I'd like to sit up."

"Okay, but go slowly."

Annie shot around the bed and helped Jonathan sit Gran up on the side of the bed.

Gran blinked a moment and then her face wrinkled in a big smile. "It's passed. Flora Ann's tea must have helped, I think."

"Who?" Jonathan asked.

"That's me," Annie said and tried to look everywhere in the room but at Jonathan.

"Oh."

Gran stood up before either of them could stop her. Jonathan opened his mouth to speak, but Gran spoke ahead of him. "Hand me my cane, Flora Ann."

The tone of authority had returned to Gran's voice, and Annie found herself doing as told without question.

"Now, hold on," Jonathan said. "You should rest."

"Tch, I've rested most of the morning away. Me spell's passed, it has. Now let me make you two some lunch."

Without waiting for an answer, she headed towards the kitchen. Although still limping, she moved more quickly than Annie had seen her move in a while. As Annie followed her, she could hear Jonathan putting his instruments into his bag.

He soon joined them in the kitchen, coat and bag in hand. "I have to get back to the office. I rescheduled my next two patients so I could come right away."

Gran leaned on her cane and looked up at him. "I'm so sorry to have troubled you."

"It's okay," Jonathan said. "But if you get dizzy again, sit down right away and call me. You hear me?" His voice was firm.

"Aye, Doctor. I will."

He left without a glance at Annie, for which she was both grateful and disappointed. What had happened in the bedroom now seemed like a dream.

When the door shut behind him, Gran stared at it, her eyes slightly glazed. "Be patient with him, Flora Ann. He's sensitive.

This was the second time Annie had heard this. "What do you mean?" she asked.

But Gran appeared not to have heard as she opened the refrigerator door and peered inside.

Annie stepped closer and in a louder voice asked, "What do you mean, Gran?"

Gran gave her a smile. "I mean to make you and Dette lunch. How's about we makes some fresh biscuits to go with those cabbage rolls from last night? You call Dette and tell her I'm fine and don't be late for lunch."

Suppressing a sigh, Annie went to fetch her phone. Once in the bedroom she lingered a moment, trying to recall what she had seen in Jonathan's eyes. If he was so sensitive, why couldn't he sense the effect he had on her?

Obviously he was sensitive about something else.

Or someone else.

CHAPTER EIGHTEEN

Annie sat up in bed. Her heart pounded in protest to the abrupt awakening by the sound of a pot crashing to the floor. Then, she smelled bacon. Her now alert ears picked up muffled giggles and low voices. Gwen and Dette must be up.

She nestled back beneath the still warm quilts, seeking sleep and eager to return to her dream about Gran that had probably been prompted by the episode at Gran's place earlier that week.

She had dreamt that Gran had been sitting in her favourite chair, stitching a quilt with smooth, young hands. "Kweel atch," she had said, grinning as if so very pleased with herself. She studied her handiwork a moment before she locked bright blue eyes onto Annie's. "Be patient with him, he's sensitive." Then with a giggle she resumed her stitching so quickly her hands were a blur. "Aye, 'tis kweel atch! So grand!"

Annie pulled at her mind, but couldn't recall any more of the dream. What the hell was kweel atch?

No longer sleepy, Annie headed down to the kitchen

to find Gwen armed with a spatula at the stove while Dette cradled a coffee mug at the table.

Gwen waved the spatula in greeting. "Sorry if we woke you. How do you like your eggs?"

"Over easy, thanks, and just one, please." Annie joined Dette at the table and poured herself a glass of juice.

Dette looked purposely at Annie, then at Gwen, and back to Annie with an expression that said, 'Isn't she wonderful?' but aloud she asked, "No further word from Wee Denny?"

"No, and he prefers to be called Dennis."

"And when might we see Dennis grace these premises again?" Gwen conducted an unseen orchestra with her spatula to accentuate her false British accent while Dette laughed dutifully.

"We won't," Annie answered. "And not because he's allergic to cats, which is reason enough."

"How come?" Gwen asked as she set down a plate of perfectly cooked bacon for which both Annie and Dette reached.

Annie swallowed a bite of bacon before answering. "I don't think I'm ready to date yet."

"Bullshit," Dette said. "You're just not ready to date someone other than Jonathan."

"Jonathan?" Gwen slid perfect over-easy eggs onto plates in front of Dette and Annie.

"As in Dr. Jonathan Dooley." Dette leaned over the table towards Annie. "See? I haven't spilled the beans."

"Yet," Annie said.

As if to prove her right, Dette continued, "Annie and he had a thing going until she found out he was still seeing his old flame in Edmonton."

Gwen joined them at the table. "Well, there's probably hope for you. Long distance relationships don't pan out. I found that out the hard way."

Annie reached for a piece of toast. "Well he's still flying out to see her on a regular basis and I refuse to be the other woman."

"Antsy, you can't be the other woman if they're not married or engaged." Dette bit off a piece of bacon and spoke around it. "You'd just be another contestant. There's nothing wrong with that."

"Yes there is if she doesn't even know she has competition."

"That's easy 'nough to fix." Dette chewed and swallowed. "Give the guy a chance, Antsy."

This reminded Annie of her dream. "You sound like Gran. That day she was dizzy, she told me to be patient with Jonathan and that he's sensitive. In my dream last night, she said the same thing."

Dette became so still that she looked frozen. Only her mouth moved when she spoke. "You dreamt of Gran? Last night?"

"Yeah, she was quilting. She looked so happy."

"She was quilting?" Dette's voice rose in both pitch and volume. She lunged to her feet and upset her coffee, half of which poured into her plate while the other half spread its dark color across the Formica tabletop. "Me phone! Where's me phone?"

Gwen reached into her jeans and thrust hers at Dette. "Here, use mine. It was just a dream, Dette. I'm sure Gran's all right."

"But she was quilting and she's not done that for years. Oh fuck! She's not answering! Fuck, fuck, fuck! Pick up the fuckin' phone, Gran!"

Gwen draped an arm around Dette. "Easy now. When was the last time she actually answered the phone? Just three days ago, you were so worried and for nothing."

Dette's shoulders relaxed a bit and her eyes lost some of their wildness. She took a breath. "Yeah. Yeah. But

I've got this aweful feeling. I'd best go check on her."

Gwen threw her spatula into the sink. "I'll take you." She turned to Annie. "Sorry to leave you with such a mess."

Annie waved. "Don't be silly. Go. Dette, call me after you get home."

Dette gave her a tight smile as she pulled on her coat. "Best I get home anyway. I'm liable to get heck if she wakes up and discovers I didn't come home at all last night." She gave Gwen a pointed look. "And I'd better arrive in my vehicle. You can follow me home if you want."

"I want," Gwen said with such tenderness that Annie felt a pang of envy.

"Then let's get the fuck home. I'm as skittish as a hen in a fox den. I hope to Jesus this panic shit is not another symptom of fucking menopause."

Gwen's answering laugh faded as she shut the door behind them on their way out.

In the startling silence that followed, Annie looked at the remains of breakfast on her plate. Her appetite vanished as her dream returned to her with an alarming clarity. Gran's clear blue eyes should have been an opaque opal. Her smooth young hands were performing a skill long ago taken away by gnarling arthritis. And that phrase, kweel atch? Or was it keel watch?

Annie wished she had Internet or had purchased a smart phone like Dette had suggested. She glanced at her own watch. The library would be open soon. And Annie planned to be on its doorstep when it did.

* * * *

Annie frowned at her quiet cell phone and had to bite hard to keep from using Dette's favourite word. She hadn't heard from her friend and each time Annie called she got put to voice mail.

She didn't want to call Dette at home, as she should be at work by now and Annie didn't want to bother Gran, who probably wouldn't answer the phone anyway.

Then she glanced at the other reason she wanted to swear: the library computer. None of her many searches found what she was looking for.

She sighed.

"Can I help you?" Someone whispered.

The girl looked young enough to be still in high school but her demeanor suggested otherwise. Her stiff posture and stern expression made Annie realize she must have sighed rather loudly.

Annie forced her own voice into a whisper. "I'm trying to find the meaning to a phrase. Keel Watch, or something like that. My searches have turned up every kind of watch or boat. Even sites for the late actor Howard Keel came up."

The girl frowned. "The phrase sounds Gaelic."

Annie recalled that Gran spoke Gaelic and refrained from smacking her palm to her forehead and saying 'Duh!'

"May I?" The girl pointed to the computer.

Annie vacated the seat and the girl began to dance her fingers across the keys. But several additional searches involving a Gaelic dictionary didn't reveal anything that made sense.

An older lady, one who definitely looked like a librarian, came over. "Gracie, dear, your husband is on line two." She smiled at Annie. "Hello."

Still frowning, the girl stood up. "Eunice, do you know anything about a Gaelic phrase that sounds like 'keel watch'?"

"Oh, do you mean kweel atch?"

"Maybe," both Annie and Gracie answered.

Eunice plopped her stocky frame into the chair and applied her multi-ringed fingers to the keyboard. Annie leaned over and watched her type in Caol Áit. Before Annie could point out that her fingers must have hit the wrong keys, several sites came up.

Gracie reached over Eunice's shoulder and selected the first one, then straightened up in obvious triumph.

"Caol Áit," Eunice said. "It's pronounced Kweel Atch."

When Annie realized what she was looking at, she grabbed her coat and tore off at a full sprint, not bothering to thank the women, as she could not get to Dette's fast enough.

CHAPTER NINETEEN

Annie passed an ambulance going the other way. With no lights flashing, it travelled at a reasonable speed that suggested it was apparently in no rush and with no emergency.

A lie, Annie thought. There was an emergency. There was a crisis. She could feel it throbbing through her veins and pulsing in her head.

Her front wheel ran up onto the curb as she parked in front of Dette's house. She leapt out, ran up the steps and nearly collided with Jonathan as he stepped through the front door. His expression confirmed the very thing Annie dreaded.

"No!" she moaned and pushed past him into the house.

Inside it was too quiet, as if Gran's passing had taken all life out of the home.

In the living room, she found Dette on the sofa with her head in her hands. Gwen kneeled in front of her. Dette lifted her head to reveal swollen eyes that held an anguish Annie knew all too well.

She held her arms out and Dette stood up only to

collapse into them, leaning so heavily upon Annie that it was all she could do to stay upright.

"I should've been here!" Dette wailed.

Gwen rubbed Dette's back. "You heard Dr. Dooley. There was nothing you could have done." She looked at Annie. "She went in her sleep."

Annie searched for phrases of comfort, but as she didn't know any that had ever helped her when Gil had died, she opted for a simple one. "I'm so sorry, Dette."

Dette became a dead weight and Annie feared she was about to fall over backwards when Gwen pulled Dette back down onto the couch.

Dette noisily blew into a tissue then looked up at Annie. "Tell me about your dream. Don't leave nothin' out."

Annie relayed everything she could remember.

"Kweel . . . what?"

"It's Gaelic. I went to the library. Caol Áit is Gaelic for a thin place. That's a place where the barrier, or veil, between the physical and the spiritual world is thin." Annie felt a chill dancing along her spine. "Where those in the spiritual world can communicate with the living."

Dette's eyes cleared with purpose. "I want to sleep at your place tonight."

"Of course. Gwen is welcome too."

Annie knew there were other things she would be able to help Dette with: calling her workplace, writing an obituary, or helping with the funeral arrangements. All this, she could do. What she could not do was ease her friend's pain.

Only the passage of time could take the edge off. Time did heal, just never completely.

And this kind of pain always left a scar.

* * * *

Annie surveyed the room. Everything was in order. Trays of sandwiches and sweets covered four long tables set up in the basement of the church. In one corner sat another small table with the tea, coffee, milk, sugar, cups, and saucers.

At the front of the room, near the door, a guest book was spread open beneath a collage of pictures of Gran at various ages. There were a lot of pictures, the older ones obviously from Gran's own albums but the more recent ones had come from relatives and friends.

Annie could tell by the cessation of the organ music above and the muffled words of the priest that she had lingered too long and the service had started.

She didn't think Dette would mind Annie's absence, as Gwen was with her, along with several Newfoundland relatives and what must be half of Sydney, as evidenced by the cars that filled the parking lot and overflowed into the neighbouring streets.

Still, Annie felt she owed it to Gran to attend church with her this one last time. She was able to enter quietly, thanks to the well-oiled doors. She spotted Dette's dark curls in the front row, her head bent forward as if she was in pain, which she was. Gwen draped an arm over her friend's shoulder.

There were few free spots remaining, and Annie slipped into the one at the end of the last row. She tried to focus on the priest's words, but the weight that had accosted her at Christmas returned and within minutes she had to give in to the irrational urge to flee.

Forgive me, Gran, she thought as she escaped once more the foyer. After the heavy door muted the sound of the priest's voice, she leaned against a wall and allowed her grief free rein, for Gran, for Gil, and for all the angst these walls harbored.

She sniffed, blew her nose and looked around. Was this also a "thin place"? It did feel heavy, like her house. She decided to wait downstairs for the service to end.

Perhaps she'd have a cup of tea. Gran had always told her that there were few ills a cup of tea could not make better.

As she headed towards the stairs to the church basement, she could almost feel Gran smiling and realized that by having tea, she was doing as great a homage to Gran as she would be attending the service.

* * * *

Annie, her arm linked through Dette's, carefully placed her high-heeled shoes on the uneven ground. With each step, Dette leaned more heavily on Annie's arm and she was grateful Gwen propped up Dette on the other side.

Three weeks had passed since Gran had died and the unusually mild weather enabled them to open the grave earlier than expected.

Annie was grateful this service was limited to a select few: Gran's nephew, Fred, from Newfoundland, the next-door neighbours, Gwen and Annie. And Jonathan.

She learned from Dette that Jonathan had been seeing Gran with increasing frequency her last few months, a house call being a pretense for a crib game. Or was it the other way around?

Not for the first time, Annie wished Jonathan was not such a nice guy. Then it would be easier to shove aside that tug she felt for him every time their paths crossed. It was a pull not dissimilar to what she had felt with Gil the first time he walked into the classroom.

Now, with Jonathan dressed as he was in a dark suit, the pull was particularly strong. What was it about a suit and tie that made any man look good?

Part of Annie still wanted to know the details he had offered. A larger part told her to run and run far.

After Gran's funeral, Dette had spent a lot of her bereavement leave working on Annie's house and with Gwen's help, it was nearly ready to be put on the market.

Dette frequently slept over, but as yet had no dreams of Gran. And lately, Annie had not heard the whisper. She wondered if she, like the house, was ready for a change.

Thankfully, the graveyard service was brief, as she could feel the thin spikes of her heels sinking into what was probably someone else's grave.

Only after the box of ashes was placed into the hole did Dette break down. When Gwen was unable to console her, Jonathan stepped up and wrapped his long arms around Dette. She folded into him like Annie wanted to.

After a moment, Dette wiped her tears off his jacket collar and said, "You know, I think you're the first man I've ever hugged."

"I'll take that as a compliment," Jonathan said and they all started to giggle, including the priest.

Dette sobered. "What would Gran think, me laughing over her grave?"

"She would love it," Jonathan said, "and you know she would."

"By laughing, you're celebrating not her death but her life," Gwen said.

Dette paused, her eyes glazing over in thought. "I

know Gran would have wanted the church service, but I think she would also have wanted a wake. I wish I'd have thought of it before. A kitchen party. With tons of food, and drink, and music." She looked between Annie and Gwen. "Is it too late for that?"

"No," Gwen and Annie answered in unison.

"A good idea," said Fred. "I'll borrow a fiddle. And if you can wait a few days, some of the cousins will come over from Newfoundland I knows they will."

Dette's eyes lit up. "Yes, 'tis the thing to do. A party for Gran."

Yes, Annie thought. Gran would have loved it.

CHAPTER TWENTY

Annie frowned at her image in the mirror. She looked tired. That damn ghost of a doorbell had sounded again that morning and she had been unable to get back to sleep. So what door was she supposed to be opening now?

The mirror above her dresser afforded her only a view from the waist up so she padded down the gleaming hardwood floor into the master bedroom, which she already referred to as Dette's room.

Or should she say, Dette and Gwen's? The two didn't stay over very often now, but when they did, the house felt less empty and more like a home, so she welcomed their presence.

The renovations, strangely, made the house feel emptier, as if removing the old carpets, window coverings, and wallpaper also removed some of the old memories. Good and bad, Annie thought. She took a long, deep breath. Eau de paint and floor finish. Yet, the air did not feel so heavy.

So why, with the house nearly ready for market, didn't

she feel energized? Gran's death was a factor, she knew.

Losing Gil had created a hole inside of her that would never be completely filled. Though, for a short time, that hole had not seemed quite so big when she had been attracted to Jonathan, when she felt she could fall in love again. But that was before she had learned he was still involved with someone else.

She sighed away this line of thinking and planted herself in front of the mirrored closet. Front on, blah. Though never having a weight problem, she had never had much of a waistline, even in her youth.

She turned. Her profile offered a slim physique, complimented by the shirt and snug jeans whose stretchy material made them so very comfortable. She figured whoever invented stretch denim should be given a Nobel Prize of some sort.

The shirt and jeans were her first purchase of new clothes since losing Gil. As she had lost a bit of weight with hockey and the house renovations, her other clothes now looked baggy on her.

Dette insisted the notice for Gran's wake specify casual dress only and include a warning that anyone wearing anything otherwise would not receive bar tickets.

Annie had lots of casual clothes in her closet. But Jonathan would be there. And in spite of her reservation to stay away from the man, she wanted to look nice. She frowned and placed her hands on her hips. No, to be honest, she wanted to look hot. And hot she was not.

Everything was for the best, she told herself. Else she might be tempted to actually stay here in Sydney. Gil's meager pension and CPP payments barely covered taxes, utilities and insurance with a bit left over to live on but there was nothing left to pay down the loan she had taken out for the renovations.

Another possibility wedged into her mind: she could

get a job and refinance the loan for a longer period. She pictured herself in a Tim Horton's cap, growing grey and plump from the ready source of carbohydrates that she craved on a regular basis.

No, she should sell the house, return to Toronto, find a tiny apartment out in the suburbs, and perhaps get a job teaching English as a second language. She could re-establish the friendships she had forged through hockey and her writer's guild.

A door slammed below.

"Antsy!" Gwen had adopted Dette's favorite moniker for Annie. "You ready?"

Annie scurried down the stairs. "Thanks for picking me up." Gwen had offered to chauffeur both Dette and Annie this night, allowing them to drink.

"My pleasure," Gwen said. "It'll be worth it to see both of you plastered. Dette's waiting out in the car." She darted back outside, her words and her actions telling Annie to get a move on.

Annie reached for her coat, planning to start on the alcohol as quickly as possible before the grief of Gran's passing and the memory of Gil combined to dampen her mood.

A night of celebration, Dette had declared. They would celebrate Gran's life with music, drink, and food. To accommodate the throng expected, this kitchen party was being held at the local curling rink.

So Annie intended to celebrate. Even if Jonathan was there. She sighed as she zipped up her coat.

It will be all right.

Annie started to smile, as she was beginning to welcome this whisper but she froze when the voice continued.

Be patient with him.

She tried to convince herself that the additional words

were only a memory of what Gran had said. She hurried outside and jumped into the back of Gwen's car, its warm interior unable to curb the chill worrying her soul.

As Gwen backed the car out of the driveway, Dette swiveled around and frowned at Annie. "Now, no grieving, you twit. This is a celebration, remember? We're going to drink till the room spins, then dance till it straightens out, then eat till our guts are stuffed. Just what Gran would want us to do. Got it?"

Annie forced a grin onto her features and hoped that in the dark interior of the vehicle it looked authentic. "You betcha. I wants what Gran wants."

Dette laughed. "Now yer talkin'!"

As Gwen pulled away, Annie glanced back at her house.

Caol Áit.

If such a thing as a thin place existed, then why not a thin house?

CHAPTER TWENTY-ONE

Annie was on her second glass of wine when she spotted Jonathan. The band had already been playing over an hour and she was beginning to wonder if he had decided not to come.

His jeans and soft jean shirt qualified him for bar tickets and at the same time ignited a tug of attraction in Annie, as strong as ever. She was once again tempted to talk to him, to find out why he had kissed her when he had someone waiting for him in Alberta.

Jonathan stored the guitar case he was carrying behind the band which currently consisted of three young men: one on drums, one playing lead guitar, and the third playing a stand-up bass. After three or four songs, mostly of the country or soft rock variety, another group came on stage with their guitar, mouth organ, and fiddle and played a few tunes.

Unresponsive to her command, Annie's eyes continued to seek Jonathan while she pretended to be listening to what the other hockey gals were saying. Although most of the Dames came to Gran's wake with their husbands, they had abandoned them for the company of their teammates. The men, huddled at the bar, didn't seem to mind.

The room was now filled with a myriad of people, from children to octogenarians yet only a few people hit the dance floor. Jonathan danced a few times, mostly with older women, but to this point he only acknowledged Annie's presence with a brief nod. She responded in kind, trying to snuff the hurt burning inside her. It was for the best, she told herself.

She jumped when Dette plunked her long arm over Annie's shoulder.

"Hey Antsy. Good turnout, eh?"

Annie planted her feet to support her tall friend. As promised, Dette appeared to be tying one on with the help of the shooters that everyone was handing her. Gwen, in full protective mode, hovered at Dette's side.

"A great turnout," Annie said.

"Man, Gran would've loved this. Wish I'd done a party for her before she passed, but then she wouldn't have let me. Unless I had a wake for someone she knew, then she might have come." Dette wrinkled her nose. "Then again, she hadn't gone out much those last couple of years." Dette's eyes grew moist, but then her attention was drawn to the stage and Annie followed her gaze.

The band had vacated the area and Jonathan sat on a stool with his guitar. He adjusted the microphone and then he clipped a small gadget on the end of his guitar and proceeded to tune the strings.

"Someone once told me that professional musicians tune their instruments *before* they're supposed to start," he said with a shy smile.

The pull Annie felt towards him survived the width of the room. Then, to her dismay, Dette dragged her through the crowd to right in front of the stage.

Jonathan frowned as he concentrated on tuning his guitar and even this expression Annie found seductive. It was the alcohol, she thought, and vowed to slow down.

When he finished tuning, he looked out at the crowd. "I met Gran shortly after I moved here, and," he laughed softly, "she soon put me in my place, particularly when it came to playing crib. I used to think I was pretty good at crib." He strummed softly, as if testing his tuning. "Until I played with Gran."

A ripple of chuckles moved through the crowd.

He continued to strum as he went on. "As most of you probably know, Gran was born in Newfoundland, but she moved here in her teens and spent many years on a farm bordering the Mira River.

"Last December, after dishing me out a big piece of humble pie over a crib board, Gran asked me to play this song at her funeral. Then didn't I go and forget. So I'm glad Dette's giving me the chance to sing it for Gran now."

He smiled and winked at Dette and Annie longed for the soft eyes to find hers, yet she was relieved when they didn't.

He began to sing, "Out on the Mira . . on a warm afternoon . . ." His voice was deep as each word resonated through the speakers into a room gone quiet and attentive. As he strummed, he looked down at his fingers moving along the neck of the guitar, his eyes narrowing at the higher notes.

He finished the last chorus, changing the words to, "Gran's going to be with them, I know she'll be with them again."

Annie felt her throat thicken and she could hear a few stifled sobs before applause filled the room. A few called out for another song, but Jonathan ignored them and proceeded to stow his guitar back into its case.

Two fiddlers came on stage and began a lively jig. Dette hauled Annie back towards the bar.

"Shots. I needs another shot."

The bartender had one ready for her. By its clear color, Annie guessed it to be tequila. Dette handed it to Annie but she shook her head.

"Uh uh. That will only make me sick."

"But it'll get ya drunk first and that is the objective here, me son."

"Wine'll get me there too. In fact I am halfway there now. Where'd Gwen go?"

"She went to fetch me more tequila, bless her soul, as we were about to run out."

One of the fiddlers spoke into the microphone. "This next dance will be a Paul Jones. Women, join hands in the middle. Men, make a circle on the outside."

Dette let out a whoop and tossed back her shot. "C'mon, Antsy!" She grabbed Annie's hand and before Annie could protest that she had no idea what a Paul Jones was, she found herself part of a large circle of women facing out. As there were not as many men as women, the guys facing in had to stretch their arms to complete their circle around the women.

When the music started, the women moved in the opposite direction to the men. It was a lively jig and Annie was just thinking she was getting the hang of it when the music stopped. Jonathan stood in front of a woman next to Dette who roughly hip checked the lady to the side as she pulled Annie in front of Jonathan.

Dette apologized to the lady, "I'm drunk and clumsy and Gran is probably pissed at me."

The miffed look on the woman's face disappeared at the mention of Gran.

The music started and each of the men gathered the woman in front of them in their arms for the waltz.

Jonathan hesitated. "You don't have to if you don't want to."

In lieu of answering, Annie picked up his left hand in her right. She had never danced a round waltz before but Jonathan obviously had and she found it easy to follow his one-two-three steps.

His right hand burned into her back as it guided her while he stepped around in one direction and then after a few more steps, in the opposite direction, all the while steering her around the room. She looked everywhere but up at him and concentrated on where he was leading her.

But he was good at this dance and the others were too. Even though the floor was filled with rotating couples, there were no collisions.

Annie relaxed into the beat and began to enjoy the dance, although something at the back of her mind told her she was enjoying it a little too much and that wine and physical contact with Jonathan was a dangerous combination.

The dance ended but he did not let go of her hand and she was now reluctant to protest. The fiddlers exploded into a polka and Jonathan once more wrapped his hand around her waist.

She pulled back a bit yet didn't let go. "I don't know how to polka."

Soft brown eyes held hers. "We'll take it slow."

At first she had to watch his feet, which she preferred, as she knew she could offer no resistance to his eyes. After a moment, when she was sure her feet were doing what she needed them to do, he led her around the floor more quickly and somehow they managed to not bump into any of the other couples.

Just when she was feeling a little confident, he picked up the pace and added in a spin.

This is damn fun, she thought and could not help but

smile. But that was a mistake, as he returned her smile and she was hooked and swallowed the line and sinker. She wanted him, dammit. But he was already taken.

When she first fell for Gil, his marriage was already dissolving, and he did everything he could to expedite the process, proof that he reciprocated Annie's feelings for him. This man, on the other hand, obviously did not want her bad enough to end things with Vivian.

When the music stopped, Annie tried to summon enough resolve to walk away but failed when he held onto her hand.

Three young fellows replaced the fiddlers and immediately began with "Unchained Melody." Jonathan pulled Annie into his arms and, fueled by the alcohol, she melted against him, insisting to herself that there was no harm in enjoying this short moment and that it didn't need to lead to anything more.

She leaned her head against his chest and he rested his chin on her head. His body heat melded with hers. It felt so damn good, so damn right, surely he must feel something for her.

The song ended and she looked up into eyes that confirmed he did want her and her last thread of common sense snapped.

"Tell me about Vivian."

He led her out of the room and to the very back of the cloakroom.

Without letting go of her hand, he leaned back against the wall and bent his knees just enough so that their faces were not far apart. If she wanted to kiss him all she had to do was lean forward. Instead, she took a small step back.

He cleared his throat. "I met Vivian six years ago. She was a social worker at one of the hospitals I had privileges at in Edmonton. We met at a function and got talking, and, well," he cleared his throat again, "she had been divorced for several years and raised her two children on her own. It wasn't until her kids went off to university that she allowed herself to date.

"A year after we started dating, we moved in together. Then, three years ago, when I decided to move here to see my grandchildren grow up, she left her job and came with me. She absolutely hated it here, even after we moved into the new house. Then last year she was offered a promotion back in Edmonton, and," he sighed, "she moved back and we thought we'd try the long distance thing."

He shook his head. "It didn't work. Lately, I haven't been flying out as often and she hasn't been down here in months." He looked at Annie, his eyes soft with sadness. "It's going to end."

But when? Annie wanted to ask. She searched for the emotional detachment of logic, but as that had dissipated with that last dance, she grasped for morality. "She doesn't know about me, does she?"

He shook his head. "No." He raised his eyes to meet hers. "Vivian was abandoned by her husband. She sacrificed her life for her kids." He took in another breath and let it out slowly. "I don't want to be the one to end the relationship."

"Alrighty then." Annie turned to leave.

"Annie, wait."

The gruff emotion in his voice made her hesitate.

He reached for her wrist and gently turned her back around. "I'm absolutely certain Vivian *is* going to end it. I just want her to be the one to make the decision. She's had enough abandonment. I don't want to add to that by telling her I've found someone else. Someone I want to be with." He lowered his head until their noses were nearly touching. "Someone I can't stop thinking about."

His breath from these last words caressed her mouth,

and Annie found herself leaning forward. Just before their lips met, she leaned back and studied his face. He was not lying to her.

Uncertainty scrambled Annie's thoughts. As Dette would say, he wasn't married or engaged. They were two consenting adults. But . . . he would be cheating on Vivian if anything happened between them. And that was a moral line that Annie could not cross.

"There's no way we can move forward until you've ended it with Vivian. We could be friends, but anything looking like a date is off limits."

He nodded. He straightened up and sighed. "Then I guess we shouldn't linger in the cloak room."

She turned and went out, feeling the distance growing between them. Regret flushed through her at the thought of no more dances with him.

But when she entered the hall there was no music and no dancers on the floor. Instead, people lined the windows, looking outside. She wedged herself next to Dette and peered through the window.

Winter had decided to return and crash the party. Wind-tossed snow nearly obliterated the parking lot.

Right away the more senior of the guests began to head home. Others soon followed and before long only a handful of friends were left. Dette told the bartender he could close up.

"Too bad about the weather, Dette," Annie said. She could feel Jonathan hovering nearby.

Dette waved her words away. "Nah. It was a great party. I'm a little more sober than I'd planned, but maybe that's Gran's way of sayin' hello."

Dette then turned to Jonathan. "Best you be on your way, too. Would ya mind dropping Annie off home for us?" Without waiting for a response, she followed Gwen into the cloakroom.

Annie exchanged a glance with Jonathan and was about to say she would get a cab home when Jonathan stepped close.

"Almost everyone's gone home. It should be okay to get a ride from a friend in a storm."

The storm did provide a bit of a cover. Outside in the parking lot, everyone else was either bent over against the pulsing snow pellets or busy clearing their windshield.

A strained silence persisted on the ride home, and not because of the slick conditions. The snow had eased some by the time Jonathan pulled into her driveway and Annie hoped it would soon turn to rain.

She wished things were different and she could ask him in to spoon with her while the storm serenaded them to sleep. But she knew that would be crossing the boundary they had just set.

She looked at him and found he was frowning at her house.

"What's wrong?" she asked.

He sighed and looked back to her. "I'm worried."

"About what?" Telling Vivian the truth? she wanted to ask.

He paused a moment, as if deciding what to say. "I'm worried you'll sell your house and move back to Toronto before we get a chance."

She resisted the urge to smooth the crease between his eyebrows. "It's still not ready yet to put on the market." She didn't add that it could happen within a few weeks. Or that he could choose to tell Vivian now.

He turned to her. "Can we go to dinner sometime? As friends?"

"No. Out of respect for Vivian, we can't do anything that would look like we're dating."

"I understand," he said softly. "Would it be all right if I called you sometime? To chat?"

"Sure."

Before she could give him her cell phone number, he rattled it off with a grin. "Dette gave it to me right after you got your phone. But I didn't want to call you until you told me I could."

Dammit, why did he have to be so nice? She got out and splashed through wet snow to the porch.

He didn't back his vehicle out until she opened the front door. She waited in the doorway until his taillights disappeared around the corner. Was he going to call? Or was this the last time she would see him?

Gil and she had lots of opportunity to see each other while he waited to finalize his divorce: classes, seminars, academic functions. And they had talked each day on the phone. While they waited, they had managed to stay connected. But how could she stay connected to a doctor when the only activity they had in common had ended for the season? Had she just done something really, really stupid?

She stepped inside and listened.

Silence. No whisper telling her it would be all right. Just before she headed up the stairs she heard a gentle tingle. Its foreignness made her pause. Then she realized it was coming from her coat. The caller id sent her heart racing.

"Hello?"

A soft laugh, then, "You said it would be okay if I called."

"I hope you're not driving."

"Yes, but I have Bluetooth." After a long moment of silence, he said, "Well, I should let you go to bed."

"Okay," she said. She waited, hoping that by doing so she could extend the conversation.

Another long pause followed, then he said, "I might be watching the Habs playoff game Wednesday night.

Want to chat during the game?"

The answer came easily. "I do."

"Okay, I'll call you after it starts. Good night."

"Goodnight," she repeated, then listened to make sure he had hung up.

As she flossed her teeth, she realized she had no way to watch the game on television. Cable. She had to get cable installed before Wednesday.

If only to watch hockey.

CHAPTER TWENTY-TWO

Annie opened the front door to Dette and Gwen. They each held a paper bag that emitted the delicious aroma of Chinese food.

"We figured it was safe to come in as Jonathan's car isn't in the driveway." Dette kicked off her sneakers and headed toward the kitchen. As she set her bag onto the table she arched an eyebrow. "So, what's the latest?"

"Jonathan and I are going to be just friends until Vivian breaks up with him."

"That's bonkers. Why hasn't he broken up with her already? Or doesn't he have the balls to do it?"

"Hush, Dette. We brought lunch," Gwen said to Annie, as if in apology for Dette's bluntness.

"Jonathan has his reasons. Pretty good ones," Annie said. "And I'm okay if we try the friend thing first." She peered into the bags. "Yum! I'm starving and I haven't had Chinese in weeks!"

They sat around the small table, ingesting their lunch in a silence threaded with an unseen tension. Annie felt not so much a premonition as a sense of something she couldn't quite understand.

Gwen and Dette's movements were quick, purposeful. The air was not heavy, but . . . blossoming. She wondered if this thin house was making her more sensitive to others. She started. Sensitive. That was the word Gran had used for Jonathan.

Annie then noticed the repeated glances between Gwen and Dette.

Annie punched Dette on the arm. "Out with it."

Dette sighed and then looked at Gwen, who nodded and said, "We have something to ask you."

Annie knew by the solemn expression smoothing Dette's usually animated features that the topic at hand was a serious one and worried that her all-is-well feeling was off the mark. So much for being 'sensitive.' "Shoot."

Dette inhaled quickly, then blurted, "Gwen and I are thinking of fixing up Gran's place. You know, brand new basement, gutting the whole main floor. Maybe even puttin' on a back deck."

"That's great. I could help with the painting."

"Yep . . . sure," Dette said. She sighed. Gwen's eyes roamed about the room, as if she, too, was nervous about what Dette was about to say.

"Out with it!" Annie ordered.

Another sigh, then: "Can we move in here with you? You know, whilst we're working on Gran's house? Laura, Gwen's room-mate, well, her lease is up, and she's moving in with her boyfriend and Gwen was thinking of moving in with me and then we thought we'd fix up Gran's house." In her haste all her words ran together, and it took a moment for Annie to digest what Dette had said.

Then Annie laughed. "Is that all? Christ, you had me worried. Of course you can move in with me."

"But, Antsy, we want to do most of the work

ourselves when we're not workin' so it'll probably take close to a year before we can move back home and with you horny to sell this place, can you actually wait that long? Do you even want to?"

A year? Annie really wanted to help Dette. And this did open a window of time for things to develop with Jonathan. Or end. Either way, if she planned on staying that long, she should look for work. She then noticed both Dette and Gwen leaning forward in their chairs, anxiously waiting for her response.

"Sorry, I got side-tracked. Of course I want you to move in. Today! Right now."

"We will pay you rent," Gwen said.

"Oh no, I don't think so."

This time Dette punched Annie, a blow much harder than the one Annie had delivered. "You twit! You can use the rent money to pay down your loan."

Before Annie could vocalize another negative response, Dette waggled a finger in front of Annie's nose. "If you are willing to postpone selling this place, the least we can do is pay ya rent."

"Dammit, Dette! I couldn't have afforded to fix this place up even with the loan if you hadn't done most of the work and gotten me the materials at a discount. The least I can do is give you a roof over your head while you renovate your place."

Gwen was about to speak, but Dette waved her to silence before hardening her features into a stubborn expression Annie was all too familiar with.

"I knows you'll give us a deal on the rent and that is plenty help enough. Besides, I will take you up on the painting offer." She looked at Gwen, "Antsy's a kick-ass edger."

Dette turned back to Annie. "But are you sure you're ready to stay here that long? When ya first came all I

heard was Toronta this, Toronta that." Her lips twitched
as if holding back a grin. "Or has it changed to 'Jonathan
this' and 'Jonathan that'?"

Annie could not help but smile. "Let's just say that
right now, I'm happy to stay here." Very happy, she
thought as she sipped her tea.

Dette leaned over the table and asked in a
conspiratorial whisper, "Even if'n you and Jonathan
never get to be more than friends?"

"You don't have to answer that, Annie," Gwen said in
the same tone she probably used to tell a perp they had
the right to remain silent.

Dette slapped the table. "Okay, I'll let that drop for
now. So, when can we move in?"

To which Gwen sighed and said, "Annie, if you want
to think about it . . ."

Annie held up a hand. "I don't."

"Are you sure?" Gwen asked, her face pinched with
concern.

Annie smiled. "I am so very sure."

She started to get up from the table, but Gwen
grabbed her hand to keep her from leaving. "If you
change your mind, or if, God forbid, things don't happen
to work out with Jonathan and you want out of here, or if
you just get tired of having us in your face, promise me
you will tell us. Promise me."

Annie returned the hand squeeze. "I promise. I'm
thrilled you two want to live here. This house is thrilled."
Love within these walls was just what this thin house
needed, she thought. "Now go start bringing your stuff
over."

Dette turned to Gwen with a grin that covered her
face. "Isn't Antsy the bestest?"

* * * *

Two weeks and several phone calls later, Annie found herself looking at a stranger in the mirror.

She had just had her hair dyed and styled and it had more body and shine than she had ever seen. She was wearing a black dress with the empire waist that made her look slim, even from the front. And heels. Higher than she'd ever worn.

Yep, she had splurged, all for this one evening. She was going to a fundraiser to support research to fight ovarian cancer. It included a dinner and silent auction. Jonathan had insisted on buying her ticket, which left her a little to bid on something at the auction.

She felt guilty at the amount she had spent but rationalized that she hadn't spent anything on herself since Gil died. She deserved this, didn't she?

A long low whistle came from the doorway. "Mighty fine, girl!" Dette said.

"Thanks to Gwen for shopping with me," Annie replied.

"Well, the lass does have good taste, she does," Dette said, then chortled. "She's waiting on ya in the driveway."

"It's so nice of her to drive me."

"She'll also see ya home safe. Just call her cell."

Gwen dropped her off at the Cambridge Suites downtown. Annie deposited her shawl at the coat check and then wished she hadn't as the air inside the lobby felt cool. Her goose bumps were probably very visible.

She peeked inside the ballroom. No one was seated yet. Her stomach tightened. Jonathan had only asked her two days ago and with her ticket so recently purchased, chances were she would be seated with a bunch of doctors or politicians she would have nothing to say to.

But she had come hoping to get a glimpse of him and perhaps a smile, a nod, or even an exchange of a few words.

She looked down the hallway and noticed a line of tables sporting various auction items for sale. A security guard stood nearby checking tickets.

A few feet past him she spotted the bar. Yes. A glass of wine was just what the doctor ordered.

Glass in hand, she followed the cue of the others and walked along the tables and discovered why a security guard had been posted.

All the items looked expensive: fine china, jewellery, paintings, sculptures, and at the end, a signed, leather-bound copy of Alistair MacLeod's *No Great Mischief*. Looking at the suggested prices, she knew she couldn't afford anything here. But she had to buy something.

After another trip down the line she stopped in front of the signed novel. As a writer, she was all too familiar with the award-winning MacLeod and she knew that his recent passing made this a particularly poignant item. Three people had already offered bids. She upped the most recent one, which brought her bid to $225. She probably didn't have a chance to get it, but in the event she did, this amount did not allow her to bid on anything else.

She looked at her glass. In her nervousness she had nearly finished it in way too short a time.

"Annie, right?"

Annie looked up. Dr. Dooley stood in front of her. Dr. Sara Dooley, that is. She looked stunning in a strapless dress complimented by thick blond locks falling onto her shoulders.

"Oh hi!" Annie said brightly, relieved to see someone she knew.

"How's the knee?"

"My knee? Oh it's good!"

"That's great. So nice of you to come."

Annie wracked her brain for a possible reason to leave the scene. She did not belong here. What had she been thinking?

But before she could think of one, she felt Jonathan right behind her.

Sara looked over her head. "Hi, Dad. Look who I found. Annie. You know her from hockey right?"

His warmth enveloped Annie, so she figured he was close, but when she turned he stood a few feet away. So maybe it was the wine? A hot flash?

"Hi, Annie," he said, his voice soft like his eyes. She hadn't seen him in two weeks and she had expected him to look good. But not this good. His tux fit perfectly.

Sara saved her from trying to find words. "We should go to our table now."

Jonathan let them both precede him. Annie longed for a hand on her elbow, but settled for the closeness of him.

At the doorway, Sara pulled her ticket out. Table ten.

Annie fumbled with her clutch as dread stirred acid in her stomach. While Jonathan and his daughter waited patiently, she finally managed to open the clasp and get her ticket.

She stared at it in disbelief. "Table ten," she said and couldn't completely hide surprise from her voice.

Sara grinned broadly, and said, perhaps a little too loudly, "What a coincidence! That's great." She led the way as Annie followed and tried to ignore Jonathan's soft chuckle.

Once they were seated, with Sara sitting between her father and Annie, Jonathan immediately filled Annie's and Sara's glasses with the white wine placed on the table.

"He's my DD tonight," Sara exclaimed. "So, if you're not driving," she raised her glass in a toast, "let's drink for him."

"That I can do," Annie said and clinked her glass with Sara's.

There were six place settings at the table, and they were joined by Greg, another doctor from the clinic, and his wife Sheila. They looked to be in their sixties. As they were both hockey fans, the topic soon turned to the playoffs.

Sara said, "These two are Boston fans while Dad and I are stalwart Habs fans, so maybe we shouldn't talk hockey."

"Who are you hoping for?" Greg asked Annie.

"I'm sorry to admit I'm a Toronto fan." Once again, the Leafs had failed to make the playoffs.

"You are?" Jonathan looked genuinely surprised.

"Yep. Us Maple Leaf fans just don't learn. We stand by our team, regardless of how they perform."

Greg laughed. "Well, who are you hoping will win?"

"I have to admit, I'm becoming a bit of a Habs fan. They've been playing with a lot of energy."

"So has Boston. Have you seen any of their series?"

"Yes I have." Annie had watched a lot of hockey on television the past two weeks and talked to Jonathan for the entire game each time. They spoke so much that she had to add minutes to her cell phone plan. "Boston is such a mean team," she added.

"You mean physical," Greg said with authority.

"A stick between the legs isn't being physical. It's being dirty. The refs should be calling more."

Greg's bushy eyebrows danced upward. But before he could say anything, Jonathan laughed and said,"Don't argue with her. She knows a lot about hockey. She's a damn good player too."

Annie felt herself blush at the pride she heard in his voice.

When the waiters began to deliver the salads, Sara commented, "Oh how lovely!"

"Very lovely," Jonathan said, but he was looking at Annie and not the salad in front of him.

Annie blushed anew and was relieved that Jonathan quickly returned his attention to his plate.

The steak and scallops that followed, each plate artistically decorated with assorted sides, was delicious.

The post-dinner speeches were on the most part short and sweet, except for the attending MLA who slid in a few platforms for the upcoming election.

After cheesecake and coffee, the emcee announced that they had fifteen minutes to finalize their bids.

The room emptied as the attendees scurried out to the hallway. Sara stood up and said, "I've finished bidding, but I do have to go to the ladies' room. Excuse me."

Before she left the table she gave a quick wink to Annie.

"So she's the one who organized our sitting together?" Annie asked.

Jonathan grinned across the table at Annie. "She is. You look absolutely amazing by the way."

Annie again felt warmth return to her cheeks. As she hadn't finished the glass Jonathan had poured for her, she knew her heightened colour wasn't wine-induced.

She picked her glass up in what she hoped was a non-chalant way and took a tiny sip. "You do too."

He said nothing, but looked at her in a way that made her want to kiss him. Then she felt something nudge her toe under the table. She removed her shoe, reached outwards, and discovered he had taken his shoe off as well.

His foot was warm and caressed hers in such a way that she wished it could travel upward. But although he was tall, his leg was not long enough.

Annie giggled. "I have never done this before."

"I'm a virgin too . . . at this," he added.

"Really?" She allowed herself to flirt. "You seem awfully good at it."

"You too."

"I'm worried I won't be able to put my shoe back on without reaching down."

"Me too."

They both giggled and then abruptly stopped when Jonathan said, "Uh oh, they're coming back.

People began to file back in and Annie panicked when she couldn't find her shoe. Just as Sara returned, Annie located it and managed to slide it back on.

When Jonathan ducked down below the table, Annie choked back a giggle and ended up coughing.

"Are you all right?" Sara asked.

Annie cleared her throat and managed to croak out that she was fine.

After the emcee gave a short speech thanking the attendants, he declared that $7,500 had been raised. The audience clapped and then people started to file out. Jonathan accompanied them as Annie and Sarah retrieved their shawls from the coat-check.

"When do we find out if we won our bid?" Annie asked.

Sara answered. "You can wait in line to look at the sheet posted or you could just wait to see if the item is delivered to you with a bill."

Annie looked. There was a crowd around the tables. Thinking she probably didn't win her bid anyway, she pulled out her phone to call Gwen.

"We'll drop you off," Sara said. "We insist." She took Annie by the arm and led her out to the parking lot.

While Jonathan held the back door open for her, Annie drank in his smile before she climbed in.

"Thanks so much for the lift," she said once he and Sara were both seated in the front.

"No problem," Jonathan replied.

The moment he pulled into Annie's driveway, Sara said, "Wow, what a neat house."

Warm pleasure spread through Annie until she noticed in the rear view mirror the frown on Jonathan's face. But it was gone when he turned around in his seat.

"Thanks for coming," he said, but his eyes said more.

"Oh no, thank you. Both of you."

Once inside the door, Annie switched on the entrance light.

The antique clock on the mantel ticked loudly and she found the sound strangely ominous, as if her good times were ticking away.

She felt like giving herself a slap. She had just had a wonderful evening. But she had to admit that she wanted much more than phone calls and footsies under a table.

She paused at the bottom of the stairs and inhaled resolve. She would not let fear of something that might or might not happen prevent her from enjoying things. She would tenaciously hold onto her good moments, revel in them, and replay them.

She once again reminded herself that she should start to look for work. Or at least see what's out there just in case there arose a really good reason for her to not leave Sydney.

She mounted the stairs and headed for her bedroom, intent on reliving the evening while she waited for sleep to come.

CHAPTER TWENTY-THREE

Aunt Jessie's anger pulses from her reddened features and Annie quickly retreats out of arm's reach.

Annie has really done it this time. She had been bouncing the ball in the house, which was a no-no to start with. She'd thrown it too hard against the wall above the couch and she'd missed the rebound. The ball had bounced against the opposite wall before striking the lamp, which then tumbled off the table and onto the floor. On impact, the lamp's delicate base splintered into shards.

Jessie stands over the remains of the lamp. "Look what you've done!" She lunges forward, grabs Annie by the wrist and hauls her toward the basement.

Annie pulls back. "Noooo, I don't want to!"

"Don't make me slap you!"

Aunt Jessie has never hit her, but Annie isn't sure she won't. She also isn't sure her aunt won't push her down the stairs so she willingly goes down two steps before turning around.

Her aunt scowls down at her and looks tall and big from the top of the stairs. "And you can stay down there until I'm done my nap!"

The door shuts, and then Annie hears the metallic scrape of the latch sliding into place, the one her parents always use at night in case burglars break into the basement. Annie knows she is stuck down here until either Jessie wakes up or her parents come home, though she has no idea when either will happen.

Trying not to cry, Annie creeps down the rest of the stairs. She's been sent here before, by her parents as well as Aunt Jessie. She hates it down here. It smells funny. It's cold. The light from the two small windows cannot reach into the dark corners.

Annie sits on the bottom step and sniffs. It isn't fair! She didn't mean to break that lamp. She wishes she'd grabbed the ball before Aunt Jessie made her come down here. Then she'd have something to play with.

She also wishes Kaitlyn was still here. She wouldn't have let them put Annie in this stupid place.

Annie shivers. It is colder now. And darker. Startled, she realizes Jessie hadn't switched the light on. She runs back up the stairs and reaches for the switch, but even standing on her tiptoes, her fingers can't reach it. She pounds on the door. She yells. She screams. She pounds on the door again.

But either Aunt Jessie is asleep or just doesn't bother to answer.

Annie sits down on the top step and leans her back against the door. When the shadows grow and begin to creep up the stairs, she folds her arms on her knees, puts her head on them, and squeezes her eyes shut.

She wakes up to the world tumbling around her. With each turn, something hard smacks into her arms and her legs. Finally she comes to a stop against the cold cement floor.

Fully awake now, she realizes she has fallen down the stairs. Fallen down the stairs! This fact alone, never mind her sore knees and elbows, is enough for her to begin wailing. Every so often she pauses, hoping to hear footsteps coming to get her.

It is during one of these pauses that she hears the whisper for the first time.

It will be all right, Annie.

Someone is down here with her! Someone she can't see! She feels about and the moment her hand finds a step, she scrambles up the stairs. Although her shrill scream fills the stairwell, she can still hear the words repeated over and over.

It'll be all right! It'll be all right!

Just as she reaches the top, the door opens and there stands Aunt Jessie, bathed in a swath of light, her expression full of remorse.

"I'm sorry I didn't turn the light on," she says. "I'm sorry I left you down there so long. I'm sorry you got so scared. I'm so sorry."

Annie sat up in bed and blinked into the grayness of dawn. She turned on the lamp and relived the event that had, until now, lain dormant in the recesses of her memory. Aunt Jessie had put her into the basement for breaking a lamp and then had gone for a nap, only to awaken to Annie's screams.

After that Annie had never been sent to the basement again. Although she can remember the contrite look on Aunt Jessie's face, this is where the dream departed from reality. Annie was certain she never heard Aunt Jessie say the words "I'm sorry" once, let alone four times. In fact, Annie was certain Jessie never ever apologized, for this or for anything else.

Coal Áit, Gran had said. A thin place. Had Aunt Jessie tried to reach Annie through a dream? She listened, part of her dreading that she might hear or see her aunt while another smaller part of her wished she would.

She recalled the dream and Jessie's tortured look of genuine remorse. Even if she didn't really believe in ghosts, there was something she could do, for herself as well as for Aunt Jessie.

As it was nearly seven a.m. she figured the others would be up soon. She got out of bed, the cold floors a shock to her bare feet. She slipped on thick socks and a warm sweater and then headed down the stairs. She turned the lights on as she went, more to make sure she didn't trip than to repel ghosts, she told herself.

She padded through the kitchen to the basement door where she hesitated for just a moment. She snapped on the basement light, pushed through a wave of anxiety, and stomped down the stairs. There, she looked into every shadow in every corner, daring a ghost to materialize.

After a moment, she realized it was just a dark, empty place, though not so empty with Jessie's things piled against one wall and some of Dette's and Gwen's stuff against another.

She said to the musty air, "It's all right, Aunt Jessie. I forgive you." She searched her soul and felt the lightness of affirmation.

She lingered, listening. When there were no responding whispers, she trod back up the stairs to change into some sweats. She was finally ready to begin to sort through the stuff in the basement. The more she could get rid of, the more room there would be for Dette and Gwen's things.

Annie paused in the living room. The air still felt heavy here, a dark ache that could be the result of persisting grief from her sister's death. Or the guilt from not reconciling with her parents before they died. Or the ache of losing Gil, the pain of which was diminished to a tolerable level by what she felt for Jonathan, but still an ache that she knew would be with her forever.

She returned to the basement and tried to be quiet as she sorted Jessie's things into two piles: one to offer to Dette and the other to go to the Diabetic Association.

Her stomach rumbled just as she heard footsteps in the kitchen above her. She went up and caught Dette and Gwen kissing at the sink, Gwen in full uniform and Dette still in rumpled pajamas.

Dette threw a grin at her. "Whatcha doin' Antsy?"

"Sorting out some of Jessie's things."

"In the basement?"

Annie smiled, "Yep."

Dette looked at Gwen. "Antsy usually doesn't like going down there." Turning back to Annie she asked, "So what's changed?"

"I had a dream last night, or rather, early this morning and it helped me remember what happened. Aunt Jessie had put me down there for breaking a lamp. No," she responded to Dette and Gwen's sympathetic "awws". "I think I deserved a time out." She gave a short synopsis of the event.

"Oh, man, that must have been terrifying," Gwen said and Annie wondered if the cop realized she was using a Dettism.

"What about the whisper?" Dette asked to which Gwen said, "What whisper?"

Annie waved a hand in dismissal. "I thought I heard someone say, 'It'll be all right' after I fell and I thought it was a ghost talking to me. I ran screaming up the stairs, and Jessie finally opened the door."

Annie didn't admit to Gwen that she still heard this whisper on occasion and was grateful Dette remained quiet.

"Anyway, after I woke up, I went down into the basement." Annie spread her arms. "No more suppressed memory, no problem being down there. Finally, after what? Forty some years?"

"Did your aunt ever apologize for doing that to you?" Gwen asks and Annie thought Dette had scored big with this empathetic woman.

"Not while she was alive, but she did in my dream last night."

"Caol Áit," Dette said. "Gran may visit me yet." She leaned towards Annie. "Have you dreamt of her again?"

When Annie shook her head no, Gwen took Dette's hand. "Maybe Gran knows you're okay and she has moved on."

Annie was surprised to discover the usually no-nonsense, practical policewoman to be so spiritual. Her words made Annie wonder if she hadn't dreamt of Gil in some time because he knew she was okay.

Yet, in spite of the whisper and in spite of her dreams about Gran and Aunt Jessie, Annie still believed they were only the result of neurons firing off in a mind trying to cope with life and death. She decided that what was really important was that she was coping.

She smiled at her friends. "I can help you move more of your stuff over today, Dette. But I'm busy tonight."

"Oh, are ye now?" Dette asked with a sassy smirk on her face. "Let me guess. You've decided to get physical with the good doctor. Because he bought you that book at the auction?"

The day before, Alistair MacLeod's book had been delivered with a notice that it had already been paid for. Jonathan must have noticed she had bid on it. A timeless gift.

"No. We are still just friends. There's NHL playoffs on tonight. Now, are you making the porridge or am I?"

Dette shook her head. "You do it. I'm going to see Gwen to the door."

Annie grinned as she reached into the cupboard for oats. She would make extra as it would be an arduous day cleaning out the basement. She'd be so busy, she hoped, that time would pass quickly until her phone rang.

CHAPTER TWENTY-FOUR

The doorbell woke Annie yet again, this time from a deep sleep that had taken several hours to reach. Dammit! She knew her anger would not let her get back to sleep so she threw the blankets off and then had to apologize to a roughly-awakened Temp. Obviously the cat could not hear the doorbell.

Jonathan had not called in four days. After three wonderful weeks in which not a day passed that they did not talk.

During their last chat he had told her he was going to speak to Vivian the next time he saw her and that he was trying to arrange a trip west as soon as he could get time off at the office.

Then nothing. Annie had begun to worry if he was okay until yesterday morning when she saw his car at the clinic on the way to get groceries. So he was still in town.

Questions about Vivian had kept her tossing and turning until well past midnight. Finally Annie had decided she would wait one more day and then call him. If Vivian were still in the picture, then it would be over.

Annie could accept that, but she knew she had fallen too far for it not to hurt.

Then she looked at the clock and was shocked to see it was nearing eleven am. She had gotten over eight hours of sleep. Time for her to be up anyway.

Later this week the new windows and siding would arrive. Until they did, maybe she could help Dette and Gwen at Gran's.

After a very late breakfast, she got into her car and headed directly to the place she would always refer as Gran's.

She felt relief at the absence of cars in the driveway. She didn't feel like company and would rather work alone.

She plodded up the steps as she tried to ignore the too cheerful chirps coming from birds perched on branches sporting swollen buds.

The new steel door was unlocked, probably from out of habit rather than from the fact that there was virtually nothing worth stealing inside the house.

Although she had been at Gran's recently, she was still shocked at what she saw. Along with all the furniture and appliances, the walls had been removed, as well as the flooring, leaving an expanse of raw plywood. The only thing left from the original house was a large claw-foot tub.

Drastic, Annie thought, and wondered if this was Dette's way of coping with Gran's absence. Annie immediately recanted this thought as Dette had kept Gran's bed, double dresser, and kitchen table and chairs, which were all now stored in Annie's basement. Besides, Gran could not be so easily erased.

Annie turned up the small radio, grabbed a broom and began to sweep up some of the debris left on the floor: remnants of carpet underlay, chunks of plasterboard, a few nails, and several staples. She bent over to scrape the pile onto the dustpan when she noticed a pair of boots standing behind her. A man's boots.

With an involuntary yelp, she straightened up and spun about, losing most of the contents of the dustpan.

"Sorry," Gwen said, in full uniform, her arms laden with a bucket, sponges and a MacDonald's take out bag. "I thought you heard me come in." She set down her wares and then turned to the door as Dette blew in with her usual bluster.

"Shit, Antsy, if we'd known you were here we would've brought you lunch too." She set down the hefty toolbox she kept in her car, along with a blanket, and then turned down the radio.

Uh-oh, Annie thought, I've just crashed a picnic. And they probably only had a short while before Gwen had to return to work.

"Uh, I've finished all I can do here, anyway," Annie said. She reached for her coat, avoiding but still feeling Dette's assessing look.

"I take it the good doctor didn't call," she said.

Annie shrugged in an attempt to show disinterest but her "whatever" sounded lame to her own ears.

A gentle tingle filled in the ensuing silence and the three of them dug into their pockets for their phones. Annie's phone remained blank, empty.

Gwen spoke into hers then her eyebrows rose in surprise. "Oh shit! I forgot it was today! Yeah, just leave it there, and I'll pick it up later. Thanks, eh?" She frowned at her phone. "Shit, shit, shit."

"What's wrong?" Dette asked.

"Oh, a pal from Ottawa just flew in with my computer." She glanced at her watch. "I should have had her mail it like I wanted her to, but cheap me, when she offered to pack it up and check it along with her luggage,

I let her. Fuck! I wonder how long they'll leave it in the baggage area."

As Annie knew Gwen's shift wouldn't end until that evening, she jumped at the opportunity. "I'll go get it."

Gwen studied her. "You sure?"

"I am. What's the name of your friend and what was her flight number?"

"Marilyn Powers." Gwen pulled out a pad and pen and scribbled down the information. "Thanks so much, Annie. I really appreciate it."

"No problem." Annie hurried outside, grateful for this little errand, as she knew from experience that doing something for someone else always helped dispel dark clouds, even if only for a little while.

It was a beautiful, cloudless day and as she walked to her car she could hear water running in the gutters. The air smelled of mud and the bright sun beamed warmly.

Spring, the eternal metaphor for optimism, Annie thought.

She decided she had absolutely no reason to feel blue. She had no regrets. If the last three weeks of phone calls and that one night at the function was all she would get with Jonathan, then so be it. Better to have had that brief, wonderful time than not to experience it at all.

As she drove towards the airport, she turned the radio up and sang at the top of her lungs to the oldies, grateful no one could hear how off-key she was. The singing, the sun, and the clear roads all put her in better spirits by the time she reached the airport.

In the relatively confined baggage area of the Sydney airport, Annie easily located the cardboard box containing Gwen's computer. Soon, she pulled out of the parking lot with her prize safely belted in beside her. With the airport only twenty-minutes away, this little chore would take less than an hour.

She missed the exit and was forced to drive by the drop-off area in front of the airport. She slowed when she spotted Jonathan's vehicle. Or what looked like Jonathan's vehicle. She slowed further and there he was. He stood way too close to a tall blond dressed in an expensive suit.

What happened next Annie would play over and over in her mind and at a speed much slower than the actual event. As Annie passed them, Jonathan had his hand on the woman's arm and he leaned towards her, the tilt to his head painfully familiar. He was going to kiss her.

Annie could not stop herself from watching in the rear view mirror as he did indeed kiss this woman. This Vivian.

A yell made Annie yank her gaze forward and slam on her brakes. She had nearly run over a pedestrian. The man glared at her like she had committed the worst of crimes.

"I'm sorry," she mouthed to him as he stomped past the front of her car. As soon as he passed, she eased forward, not wanting to, but unable to stop herself from glancing in the rearview mirror. Jonathan had straightened up and was looking right at her. She stepped on the gas, and, watching for other moving objects, human or otherwise, drove away as fast as she dared.

The trip home passed in a numb haze. She had just set the box down inside the door when the ringtone of her cell phone tinkled way too merrily. She suppressed the urge to throw it against the wall, but instead checked to make sure it was not Dette or Gwen calling.

It was Jonathan. Now he decides to call, she thought. She shut off the phone and stuffed it into her coat pocket. No, it was over, definitely over. She could accept that. She just wished it didn't hurt so damn much.

She carried the box up to what used to be Jessie's

sewing room and what they now referred to as "the office".

Don't think, keep busy, she told herself. I can do this. I will do this. I don't need this man.

Then, in spite of her insistence not to, her throat choked with sobs and tears began to fall. These were not tears of self-pity, but tears of anger. Anger at allowing herself to be so stupid as to fall in love with someone already taken.

It will be all right.

"No, it won't!" she screamed to the empty house. "It will never be all right!"

She sat down on the floor beside the half-emptied box and waited. For what? An answer?

"Go ahead," she said loudly, then added on impulse, "Prove to me that ghosts do exist and that I'm not just a crazy, stupid bitch."

She fell silent and listened. The only response was the faint tick of the clock on the mantel downstairs.

Why the hell had she wanted a relationship that could only have ended in heartache? Death or departure, and taxes, were the only certainties in life.

She reminded herself that she still had several years to live and to enjoy life, although she'd give anything to have been able to give Gil some of those years. All of them, even. But she couldn't so she should just suck it up. She blew her nose. So, what did she want to do? Really do?

Not be alone, was the first answer that came to her. But she was not alone. The multitude of shoes in the entranceway, the coats weighing down the coat rack, the piles of beauty products taking up every available space in the bathroom, and the sink full of dirty dishes were all evidence that this thin house had become a home. At least for now.

She pulled a keyboard out of the box and as she

studied it an idea wedged through the gloom. She could start to write again. About some cheating asshole, perhaps. She walked into her own room and pulled down a briefcase from her closet.

She had not seen her laptop in so long that it looked foreign, almost new. She plugged it in and was thrilled by the little buzz it made when it booted up. The first file she opened was a short story she had begun about a homeless person and she could not help but laugh at the irony.

Well, she was homeless no more and before she knew it her fingers were flying as she became immersed in another world. A world in which there were struggles, but not hers. Pain, but not hers.

And there were no whispers.

* * * *

Annie sat on her bed with her back propped by pillows and her laptop on her lap when Dette appeared in the doorway.

She had her hands on her hips. "Antsy. Why isn't your phone on?"

"Because I don't want to talk to anyone."

"Oh, shit." Dette came into the room. "What's Jonathan done now?"

Annie kept typing. "I'd rather not talk about it." For at least a few hours now, her writing had allowed her to block out all thoughts of Jonathan and she wanted that to continue.

Dette waited while Annie typed, at first, coherent sentences, then just random letters and finally symbols that began to look like the swear words used in cartoons. Then the screen blurred as unwanted tears poured down her cheeks.

"Dammit!" Annie closed the laptop and covered her face in her hands. The bed sagged to the left and then a warm body sidled next to her as an arm snaked about her shoulders.

"Ooh, Antsy, you got bit bad, didn't ya?"

Annie dropped her hands and looked at the tear-blurred image of her friend. "I was so stupid. I fell for the first male that looked sideways at me. Then, even after I found out he had someone else in his life, I still wasted time with the sonofabitch. I even let myself think I had fallen in love with him. Stupid, stupid, stupid! Wrong, wrong, wrong!" She reached past Dette for a tissue and blew her nose so hard her eardrums popped. "Those were tears of anger by the way. I'm fine. Just pissed off is all."

"How about I borrow Gwen's billystick and go beat the shit out of him? Gwen will probably help. Did he call you and tell you he's going back to the Alberta bitch?"

Annie blew her nose again. "No. I saw them at the airport. Kissing. He'd told me they'd be breaking up. Argh! I was soooo stupid!"

"I see. But you know, Antsy, it's lucky you did go to the airport, else you might never have known he was a lying skank. Though I must admit I am surprised to hear this about Jonathan. It seems out of character for him."

The theme from Jeopardy tinkled from Dette's coat. She grinned. "Just programmed that baby, so's I knows it's mine." She pulled out her phone and looked at it. "Shit."

Annie stiffened. "Jonathan?"

Before Annie could blurt out for her not to answer it, Dette flipped it open. She spit "Arsehole" into the phone and then listened a moment. "Well, Sherlock, that must have been your first clue she doesn't want to talk to you. Now fuck off!" She snapped the phone shut and looked at Annie, a grin dimpling her cheeks. "How was that?"

"Perfect," Annie said, but it didn't feel perfect. It felt horrible. She reached for her laptop. "Now, if you'll excuse me, I'll do something useful, like completing this character arc for my homeless protagonist."

"Whatever that means," Dette said, "As long as yer not pining over some lying pissant. Meanwhile, I'm going down to make us all some hot rum toddies. I'll bring one up to you." She left the room, but her voice returned from the stairwell. "But don't go thinkin' this special treatment will be on-goin'. Me good will lasts only so long, then it's back to me, me, me."

Annie could not help but grin at the irony of her kind-hearted friend thinking she could be self-centered. She set her laptop at the bottom of the bed and clambered out, eager to go down and watch Dette and Gwen make the toddies and, no doubt, laugh some more.

CHAPTER TWENTY-FIVE

Gran rocks and grins, rocks and grins, her fingers a blur as the needle goes in and out of the quilt on her lap, the intricate rose taking shape at a speed that tells Annie she must be dreaming.

Annie thinks she must remember to tell Dette she has had another dream of Gran. Then she wonders that if she is indeed dreaming, how can she be thinking of things to do when she is awake?

Gran's rocker stills, and so do her fingers. Her eyes, as brilliant a blue that Annie has ever seen, demand attention.

"He is sensitive, Flora Ann, but he needs to say it here." Her facial features grow larger with each word. "Make him say it here."

It was the enlarged image of Gran's face that lingered in Annie's mind when she awoke. She sat up and rubbed her eyes. Though this action cleared her vision somewhat, it failed to clarify the meaning behind Gran's words.

The sun had not yet risen but was threatening to, according to the dull grey peeping in through the curtains. A gentle tinkle of silverware trickled up through the stairwell, the sound so subtle that she knew whoever was down there was trying to be quiet.

Thinking it might be Dette and that she would want to know about her dream, Annie pulled on her wool socks and slipped silently down the stairs.

Gwen stood at the sink, dressed for work, sipping a cup of tea.

"Hey," Annie said softly.

Gwen spun around. "Christ, you scared me! Don't you know you shouldn't sneak up on someone armed with a gun?" Her grin diminished the sternness in her tone. "What are you doing up?"

Before Annie could answer there was a thump from above, followed by other thumps of someone not happy to be awakened coming down the stairs that reminded Annie of the time she woke Aunt Jessie.

Dette emerged, her flannel pajamas rumpled with one pant leg still crumpled above her left knee. The right side of her curly head was flattened, which made her look like her head was bashed in on that side. To compliment this, her right eye was shut, the left one squinting against the kitchen light.

"Jesus-fucking Christ!" She thrust her cell phone at Annie. "Fucking Jonathan has been calling and texting every couple of hours and the twit promises to keep calling until I get you on the phone." She opened her other eye and spotted Gwen. "Oh, mornin', hon," she said, her voice several shades softer than the tone she had used with Annie.

Gwen looked at Annie who had not yet taken the phone from Dette's still extended arm. "You gonna take that?"

In response, Annie turned around and headed out of the kitchen.

Dette pounced in front of Annie. "God, Ansty, ya gotta! Even iffin it's just to tell him to fuck off. I needs sleep. Lots more sleep." She pushed the cell nearly into Annie's nose. "Take it, fer Chrissake!"

Annie took the phone and without saying a word, pushed the end button to which Dette let out a moan. "Noooooo! He's only gonna call back and I gotta work at noon! Jesus H. Christ!"

"Just turn it off," Gwen said softly as she slid by on her way to the door.

"But you might call," Dette said to Gwen, then she paused and said, "Oh fuckit." She pushed another button then tossed the phone onto the couch. After giving Gwen a peck on the lips, she stomped back up the stairs.

As Gwen closed the door behind her, Annie remembered she had forgotten to tell Dette about the dream, but decided to wait until after Dette had gotten more sleep. Besides, Gran's message had been intended for Annie.

Make him say it here, Gran had said. Make who say it here? Jonathan? He was the only one Gran had referred to as sensitive. Annie shook her head, still thick from not getting enough sleep herself.

She picked up Dette's cell, intent on putting it on the kitchen table where Dette would see it before she went into work. She ran her fingers over its smooth surface. Maybe she should call Jonathan back, tell him to stop bothering Dette. Tell him to just stay away forever. Let her get on with her life. She had things to do. Like her writing that had surprisingly come back to her like it had never left.

Grasping tightly to this tiny thread of conviction and courage, she touched the phone, but realized she didn't know Dette's code. She pulled her own phone out of her coat pocket. Jonathan's number was at the top of the list of missed calls. She entered it, then held her breath while it dialed. He picked up after the second ring.

"Annie I was saying goodbye to Vivian at the airport."

He was saying goodbye? To Vivian? Annie was about to give in to the ray of hope and urge him to go on, then remembered what Gran had said in her dream.

He needs to say it here. Make him say it here.

"If you want to talk, you know where to find me," Annie said. She quickly pressed the "end" button and then she turned off the phone. If he wanted to talk to her bad enough, he would come. If he didn't show up, then she would know for sure it was over.

Knowing she would not be able to get back to sleep, she put on the kettle. Tea, porridge, and then resume writing.

Better writing than waiting.

CHAPTER TWENTY -SIX

Annie carried the bowl of popcorn and glass of wine into the living room. Since hanging up on Jonathan that morning she had managed to pass the day writing.

She had actually completed a draft of her short story. It was her first finished product since before Gil was diagnosed.

Her protagonist overcame painful personal trauma and moved on to a more productive life. And she could too, she decided. But at the moment, she had neither the calmness of mind nor the energy to compose more fiction. Hopefully the wine and movie would keep at bay the gloom lingering at the forefront of her consciousness.

Annie would have preferred to go over to help Dette and Gwen with Gran's house, but maybe Jonathan had worked all day at the clinic and intended to come here tonight. If he did and she was not home, he might find her elsewhere and Gran had been insistent that he say it here. Whatever 'it' was.

So here she would sit and wait. For tonight anyway. If he failed to come, she would permanently erase him from relevance and follow in the footsteps of her protagonist.

She picked up the remote and selected the movie package, thankful for the cable she had hooked up to specifically watch hockey.

Before Gil got sick, he and Annie had gone to the theater often and rarely missed a movie that received good reviews. But after three years and watching hardy any movies, she now had a big selection to choose from. Surely she could find one that would prove engaging enough to keep her mind off of Jonathan.

But negative thoughts and questions managed to push through her weakened attention span. Why hadn't Jonathan called before the airport scene? Just a short message to let her know that Vivian was in town. That he was telling her he'd met someone else. That he was ending it. That he'd be driving her to the airport and saying goodbye.

Since he hadn't left any sort of message, Annie could only assume the worst. And the fact he had not yet come here to talk to her only confirmed it.

The wind picked up and blasted rain against the front windows. The foul weather, though perfect for curling up on the couch and watching television, did nothing to alleviate her downward-spiraling mood.

With a soft mewl, Temp materialized beside her and made a bed out of Annie's lap. Soon the feline emitted a soothing warmth that made Annie grateful she was not alone this night.

Then, car lights danced across the walls. Annie shut off the television in time to hear footsteps on the porch, followed by a hesitant knock that was nearly drowned out by the thudding of Annie's heart against her ribs.

She straightened out her legs from beneath her, uprooting a none-too-pleased Temp who strutted out of the room in a huff.

Before she opened the door, Annie risked a peek out the window. It was Jonathan, his hunched posture and visible frown an indication he was not happy to be here.

She steeled herself against any magnetism, any attraction, and opened the door.

He cleared his throat. "It's over with Vivian." He glanced behind her nervously. "Look, can we go somewhere else and talk?" His voice, his hands, his expression, and his posture all said *please*. He also seemed to have trouble controlling his eyes. They jerked from one side to up over her head, and then to the other side as if trying to avoid looking at anything.

Her wall of negativity, which had been steadily building higher and higher with each passing moment, began to crumble beneath his obvious discomfort. But Gran had said that he needed to say it here, in this thin house.

"No," Annie said. "We talk here." She returned to the sofa and picked up her wineglass as if to resume what she was doing, even if it meant that he would be gone by the time she turned around.

But he hovered just on the other side of the threshold. The porch kept out the rain, but the wind blew around him through the doorway.

"Shut the door," Annie said. "You're letting out all the heat." She marveled at how much she sounded like her mother.

He took a breath that reminded Annie of a swimmer about to dive into the deep end and then stepped inside. As soon as he closed the door, he leaned back against it.

In the weak lamplight he looked pale, nearly ill. He opened the collar of his shirt, as if this would allow more air into his windpipe. "I uh . . ." he gulped at the air.

Oh God, was he having a heart attack? Annie set down her glass and stepped towards him.

Then the whisper, *It will be all right.*

"Well, it doesn't feel all right!" he hissed through gritted teeth.

Annie was shocked into immobility. "You . . . you heard that?" Impossible possibilities raced through her mind.

He blinked at her, then his eyes came to rest on something over her left shoulder. He went from pale to an unhealthy white and muttered something that sounded like, "Oh, Jesus," before his legs gave way.

Annie lunged for him. She could not hold his large form up and as one they sank to the floor. In her effort to protect his head, she ended up on her butt with one knee bent beneath her and his head and shoulders resting against her chest.

Oh my God, what have I done? She could not budge him, but managed to push through the panic enough to feel his throat for a pulse. For a few awful seconds, she failed to find one. Then there it was. A bit fast, she thought but steady. His chest rose and fell in an uneven pattern.

She hugged him in relief and realized just how much this man meant to her. If only she could reach her phone in the pocket of her jacket on the hook just above her. She stretched but her fingers only grazed the hem of her jacket.

She was about to search his pockets for his cell when the whisper returned. Clearer than before. Nearer than before. As if it was coming through Jonathan.

He will be all right, dear daughter.

It sounded so close she could almost feel a breath upon her cheek.

Then, fainter now, *It will be all right. YOU will be all right.* The last word was so soft, she could have imagined it.

"Mom?" Annie asked the room.

But it felt empty. Lighter but very empty.

Jonathan groaned, then stirred, his eyes blinking rapidly as if trying to bring the world into focus.

"Hey," she said.

He pushed himself up but remained sitting beside her on the floor. Their hips and shoulders touched as they leaned back against the door. He inhaled deeply as he scanned the room, searching for what Annie knew to be gone.

She squeezed his hand. "It's all right."

He frowned at her. "What happened?"

"You passed out. Maybe I should call an ambulance." She started to get up, but he put an arm around her to keep her down.

"No. It's . . . I'm okay." He inhaled. "The air isn't so thick now." He looked at her apologetically. "I do this sometimes. A panic attack of sorts. It happens in weird places. A house. On a street. Once it happened in my son's day care."

He's sensitive, Gran had said.

She leaned into the warmth of his arm. "You heard the whisper didn't you?"

"Yeah." He frowned. "You heard it too?"

She nodded. "I've heard that whisper since I was a child, someone telling me it will be all right. I thought I was imagining it. Did you see something?"

He shook his head. "Not a thing." He inhaled slowly. "A person." His eyes were soft. "I think it was your mother, though don't ask me how I know that."

Dear daughter, the voice had said.

The last time she'd seen her mother was the day Annie left to go to university in Toronto. She'd stood on the porch watching Annie load her things into her friend's car, her face wrinkled with disapproval.

"What did she look like?" Annie asked. She wanted to

picture her mother happy and not angry, sad, or disappointed like she had that day.

"She was young. In her twenties."

"Really?" Annie asked, unable to picture her mother that young, as she had always seemed old to Annie. A thought struck her. "Wait here."

She reluctantly left him and went to the coffee table. Inside a side door were photos that she knew had always lurked there. She picked out a framed family photo. In it, she looked to be about five years old.

Jonathan joined her and she thrust the photo at him. He did not hesitate and immediately pointed to Kaitlyn standing behind Annie, her hands on top of Annie's head in a playful pose.

"That's her," he said.

"That's not my mother," Annie said.

Jonathan put a warm hand on her arm. "Oh, yes, it is," he said softly.

But . . . it couldn't be. Kaitlyn had been older than her, but not that much older. Twelve years. Maybe fourteen.

Annie went back to the coffee table and began to yank out all the albums and framed photos until she found what she was looking for: the family bible. She carried it over to the end of the couch where the lamplight was brighter and sat with it on her lap, her heart threatening to jump out of her rib cage and step dance across the room.

A curious Temp hopped up on onto the bible, sniffing the leather binding. Jonathan lowered himself down beside Annie, gently pulled the feline onto his lap, and began to stroke her and talk to her softly.

The warmth of Jonathan's nearness, his actions, and Temp's approving purr calmed Annie enough to focus on the long list of births and deaths on the inside cover of the bible. They dated back to the 1800s, all hand-written, and by at least three different people. At the bottom was written Flora Ann MacInnis. Born March 4, 1963.

"That's me," she said to Jonathan. Annie moved her finger up to the next line. Kaitlyn Louise MacInnis born June 3, 1948 and squeezed in below that: Died August 21, 1973. Goosebumps popped up and multiplied along Annie's neck. "She was fifteen when I was born." So young. Yet . . . old enough.

Jonathan nudged her shoulder with his. "You okay?"

Annie looked at this kind man and was nearly overcome by an urge to have him hold her. She realized then that he had begun to glance nervously around the room.

"Look," he said. "I don't want to leave you here alone, but this place . . ."

"Caol Áit," Annie said.

He frowned.

"It's a thin place. A place where the veil separating the living world and the spiritual world is thin."

He blew air out slowly and nodded. "So that's what it is." He looked at her, worry etching his features. "The air is lighter now, but," he looked around, his shoulders tensing. "It's still thick. Or thin, whatever. Sometimes when this happens to me, more begin to show up." He closed his eyes and inhaled slowly, roughly.

Temp chose that moment to bolt from his lap and disappear from the room in a blur. Jonathan stood up and Annie set the bible down and stood also, knowing it would not be fair to ask him to stay.

He faced her and gently grasped her arms. "Come with me."

Hope glimmered briefly at his plea, but her mind was cluttered with what she had just learned. She shook her head. "I need to try to sort this out."

"I understand." Worry returned to his eyes. "You'll be

okay if I go?"

She nodded. "This is my home."

He cradled her face in his large, warm hands and looked deep into her eyes. "That day at the airport, I was saying goodbye to Vivian. But I'll wait for you to call me. Whenever you feel ready." He didn't kiss her, but his eyes did.

When the door closed behind him, Annie returned to the coffee table and picked up the family photo again. Kaitlyn grinned out at her. She seemed so happy. And so did the child who leaned back against the teen's legs, trusting they would hold her up.

Annie knelt down beside the coffet table, it's cabinet a mountain of memories and started examining each photo, seeing it with new eyes.

"Our miracle baby," Kaitlyn had called Annie more than once and obviously at a time when Annie was old enough to remember, so not a baby.

Annie also remembered Kaitlyn calling her a Newfoundlander, as that was where she'd been born; they'd lived there a year while their father worked in a lumber camp and came home to Cape Breton the following spring with a baby. A change-of-life baby, Annie remembered being called, but really a cover-up for a shameful event.

Annie slid back and leaned against the couch as more memories flooded her already crowded brain. Arguments between Kaitlyn and her parents, particularly the one before Kaitlyn left for Toronto.

After Kaitlyn's death, Aunt Jessie moved into Kaitlyn's old room. Annie recalled not liking that at all.

Then, when Annie reached puberty, verbal battles once again filled the house between a maturing teen and parents who must have been so frightened history would repeat itself.

Annie ran her hands over a more recent family photo, one taken at a wedding. Her grandparents looked exactly like what they were, grandparents, their smiles grimly fake. She herself, looking all of sixteen or seventeen, did not even make the effort to smile or hide the anger boiling within her.

Annie studied the faces of her grandparents. In trying to control her, they had done what they thought had to be done. But they had lost her to a university in the very city that had claimed their only child.

Jessie must have known, too, Annie thought, and also tried to help keep Annie on the straight and narrow. She wondered why Jessie hadn't told her the truth after her parents died. Then again, Jessie may have been sworn to silence and it would have been her nature to uphold a promise.

Annie listened. It was the silence in the room that made her stand up and look about, searching for the source of soundlessness. Then she saw it.

The clock. It had fallen silent once again. And like so many years before, it had stopped at ten minutes after ten. At exactly the same time it had stopped before? How could that be?

An involuntary shiver pushed yet another memory at her: her father standing in front of the mantel, opening the clock face and adjusting the time. Or freezing it, Annie now thought. At ten after ten. It must have been either the time of Kaitlyn's death or the moment they first heard she'd died.

He had turned back around and told Annie to sit on the couch. Both he and her mother then sat on each side of Annie and told her that she would never see her sister again.

So they endured the heartache of losing their only child and pushed on with the task of raising Annie as their own.

Annie let out a long sigh. Her grandparents and Jessie had only been trying to do what they felt was right, and Annie wished she could have known; she might have understood their iron rule.

She clutched the photo taken at the wedding to her chest and breathed forgiveness, knowing she would never know for sure if her grandparents and her aunt could sense her understanding or her gratitude for what they had tried to do.

She set the photo down and picked up a picture of Kaitlyn at her high-school graduation. She was a beautiful young woman, happy and full of life.

"Mom?" Annie whispered then listened, praying for a response.

But there was no whisper this time saying it would be all right. Because things were all right.

And it was this that made Annie cry.

CHAPTER TWENTY-SEVEN

Annie leaned against Jonathan's vehicle in the clinic parking lot. The clinic had just closed and any minute now he would be coming out. Though a chilly wind nipped at her skin, the strengthening sun felt warm on her face.

A bird chirped cheerily and she looked up into the birch tree above her, but its newly opened leaves hid the singing bird. Although she could not see the bird, it continued its song.

Three weeks had passed since Jonathan came to Annie's house. As he promised, he had waited for her to call him. But she had not been idle.

She spent the first week reliving her youth, looking at every picture. Then the subsequent weeks passed while she recorded every memory, good or bad, on her computer. She wasn't sure why she felt compelled to do this, as she would most certainly not be sharing it with anyone. Perhaps just to put her life in perspective so that she could come to some decision as to her future.

Her memoir ended with the years she spent with Gil,

which didn't take as long as her childhood. With Gil, it had all been good until he took sick.

She now knew now that she had fallen not only for Gil but also into him. He had offered her everything she hadn't had here at home: total acceptance, unconditional love, and a security that she took for granted.

But Annie knew now that because she gave herself so totally to Gil, when he passed her world had disintegrated with only a small piece of her still existing. What had complemented her existence in Toronto, her writing, her hockey, could not sustain her once Gil was gone.

Here, she had undergone an evolution, mostly because of the house she had fled as a teen. Its equity gave her a chance for financial stability and its memories healed wounds inflicted long ago. It opened its doors to friends she needed and who, in the end, needed her.

She decided this was where she wanted to be. Writing had already pulled her back into its web and each day she looked forward to the two hours she promised to spend at her computer.

But she needed a job. At least a part time one. She sent off resumes to schools and the local university and put an ad in the paper for tutoring English. Already she had an interview scheduled for next week.

Then, that morning, the doorbell had awoken her once more. She didn't know if it was Gil or someone else telling her to move on, but she now felt she was ready, which was why she was here. This was the door she was ready to open.

And now, exiting the clinic was the person she had resolutely kept from being relevant in her decision to stay. If things worked out, he would be the icing on the cake. If not, she would still have the cake.

Three weeks had passed, which was time enough for him to have given up on her. He could already be seeing someone else. Kissing someone else.

When he spotted her, his face erupted into a brilliant grin. Without even a glance to see who was watching, he wrapped one arm around her, pulled her closely, and kissed her deeply.

He pulled away only an inch. "Where the hell have you been?" he asked in a hoarse whisper.

She pushed him back to make it easier for her to make eye contact. "I've been busy making decisions. There's one last thing to clear up."

"Oh?" His eyes grew serious.

"Do you still have feelings for Vivian?"

He didn't look away. "Yes, I do and probably always will. But not enough to move back to Edmonton. Her life is there and mine is here. She came here to tell me we should end it. To move on and see other people."

Annie believed him. But she needed to know more. "So what if she hadn't wanted to end it? What did you expect me to be? A fill-in between trips to Edmonton?"

He shook his head. "No. I knew it was going to end with Vivian or I wouldn't have given in to my attraction to you. I wouldn't have kissed you that first time." He started to pull her towards him.

She pushed against his chest and kept eye contact. "And if she changes her mind, you'll just toss me aside like a shoe that no longer fits?"

He shook his head. "No, I will tell her about you and confirm our break-up. But she won't. She flew three thousand miles to make sure she wanted to end it, and we did."

"Yeah, I was there, remember? I saw the whole thing."

Before she could stop him, he kissed her briefly on the lips. "That's a goodbye kiss," he said softly, his mouth so close that his breath mingled with hers. "This is a hello kiss." This kiss was warm, deep, and swallowed Annie's soul.

She sank against him and in spite of their jackets she could feel warmth from the whole of him. He looked down at her.

"I want you, Annie. You." He bent to kiss her again, but she put her fingers against his lips.

"But I won't share you, Jonathan Dooley. So promise me this: if you ever want to be with someone else, to kiss someone else, you have to tell me. Right away. Don't spare my feelings like you did with Vivian. I survived losing Gil so I know I can survive anything. I can handle rejection. But I will not share you. Promise me nothing but absolute truth and honesty."

His eyes held hers and did not let go. "I promise."

She wanted to add that she would never sell her house and would never become dependent on anyone else again. But this could wait. For now, she would enjoy the icing.

He must have seen a change in her features, as he asked softly, "So, am I allowed to kiss you again?"

It felt so easy to smile. "You may."

His kiss lasted so long she was about to break for air when a sharp "Hey!" made them pull apart.

Sliding by on a skateboard was a teenager. "Get a room!" he yelled as he disappeared around the corner.

Jonathan laughed softly then pulled Annie even tighter against him. "Do you want to?" he whispered, his breath tickling her mouth.

Her answer came as easily as her smile.

"I do."

And although she suspected her thin house would continue to watch over her, she knew the doorbell had rung for the last time.

THE END

ACKNOWLEDGEMENTS

First of all, thanks goes to my friend Anna Kowalski for her invaluable and ever so patient assistance with my web site and book cover. Once again I am grateful to all my 'writing buddies' in Toronto and Halifax for their support and advice with special thanks to Colleen Gareau, Carla Taylor, and Patricia Thomas. A big thank-you goes to Crystal Vaughan, my editor. And to Janice Coyle for reading both this novel and Time Tamper for me. I would also like to thank Donna Morrissey for sharing her enthusiasm and expertise in her memorable workshop. And thanks to my friends and family in Cape Breton and the island of Cape Breton itself for providing inspiration for this novel and for giving me my own personal Caper, Don, for thirty-four wonderful years.

www.ingramcontent.com/pod-product-compliance
Lightning Source LLC
Chambersburg PA
CBHW061137170626
46809CB00003B/894